"Sean Will Not Marry You!"

he said with utter conviction. "And you would not be happy with a boy," he went on in a caressing tone. "You're a woman; you need a *man*." His intent gaze left no doubt to what man he referred—himself.

He released his hold, only to pull her into his arms and Laura had one brief, startled look at his face as it descended. For a man who spoke, even obliquely, of love, he looked remarkably angry.

He pulled her roughly against his chest and, holding her immobile, kissed her thoroughly. His anger lent a sharp edge to the embrace, giving it an urgency she had not expected. That must be why her heart fluttered so disturbingly within her. . . .

JOAN SMITH

has written many Regency romances, but likes working with the greater freedom of contemporaries. She also enjoys mysteries and Gothics, collects Japanese porcelain and is a passionate gardener. A native of Canada, she is the mother of three.

Dear Reader:

I'd like to take this opportunity to thank you for all your support and encouragement of Silhouette Romances.

Many of you write in regularly, telling us what you like best about Silhouette, which authors are your favorites. This is a tremendous help to us as we strive to publish the best contemporary romances possible.

All the romances from Silhouette Books are for you, so enjoy this book and the many stories to come. I hope you'll continue to share your thoughts with us, and invite you to write to us at the address below:

Karen Solem
Editor-in-Chief
Silhouette Books
P.O. Box 769
New York, N.Y. 10019

JOAN SMITH
Caprice

Silhouette Romance

Published by Silhouette Books New York

America's Publisher of Contemporary Romance

Other Silhouette Books by Joan Smith

Next Year's Blonde

 SILHOUETTE BOOKS, a Division of Simon & Schuster, Inc.
1230 Avenue of the Americas, New York, N.Y. 10020

ISBN: 0-671-57255-5

First Silhouette Books printing October, 1983

10 9 8 7 6 5 4 3 2 1

Map by Ray Lundgren

America's Publisher of Contemporary Romance

Printed in the U.S.A.

Caprice

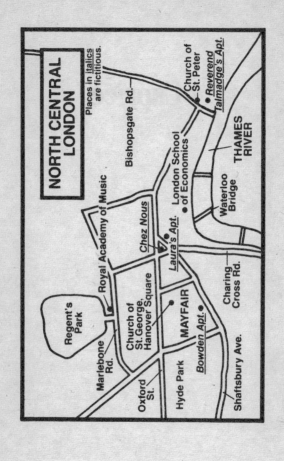

NORTH CENTRAL LONDON

Places in *italics* are fictitious.

Regent's Park

Royal Academy of Music

Church of St. Peter

Reverend Talmadge's Apt.

Bishopsgate Rd.

Chez Nous

London School of Economics

Laura's Apt.

THAMES RIVER

Waterloo Bridge

Marlebone Rd.

Church of St. George, Hanover Square

MAYFAIR

Bowden Apt.

Charing Cross Rd.

Oxford St.

Hyde Park

Shaftsbury Ave.

Chapter One

Laura Talmadge stopped and cocked her head to examine the life-size cardboard image of herself propped in the window. LOVELY LAURA AT THE ORGAN the sign said. There was no last name given, which suited her just fine. In fact it was her own idea to maintain maximum secrecy as to the identity of "Lovely Laura," who played the organ four nights a week at the dinner club called the Chez Nous. They might not like it at the Royal Academy of Music if they knew one of their star students was moonlighting at a restaurant. That it was one of the more expensive eateries in the city of London would not impress Dr. Denby, her tutor. It didn't impress Laura either, for while the proprietors, Jerry and Vera, charged a fortune, the place actually had very little chic. One was not likely to encounter the aristocracy there.

Pretentious was the word that popped into the mind upon first entering its portals. The clientele had money, but it was new money. No titled customers were to be seen, no Savile Row suits, no old school ties. An occasional celebrity from television or the movies might drop in once in a while, but that was the extent of it.

Three pedestrians passed her without remarking on any similarity between the young girl on the sidewalk, her pale blond hair covered by a kerchief against the damp air, her slender body huddled in a raincoat, and the buxom cardboard female in the display. Other than the face, there was little enough resemblance. The cardboard effigy had been created six months before to honour Aimée, the club's previous organist. When Aimée ran off with a customer, Jerry Holmes had hired Laura, and had a picture of her head blown up to stick over Aimée's ample body. Laura doubted that even Aimée had actually possessed the bosom that swelled in such abundance over the low-cut gown, then narrowed in sharply to a ridiculously small waist. The thing looked like an advertisement for a cheap movie house, but try telling Jerry that, she thought wryly.

"We want you to look sexy," he had said bluntly when she went to audition for the job. "You've got the potential there, but you don't know how to merchandise it. I'll learn you. And take it easy on that classical stuff. This is a restaurant, not a church. 'Tico Tico,' 'Ebb Tide,' the old pop favorites, that's what we play here. Our customers aren't bishops, and they're not kids either—kids can't afford my prices. I cater to a mature clientele, nobs out with their girls, and bachelors. We don't get many married couples in here."

"What do you mean, *sexy?*" Laura asked warily.

"I mean, take off those glasses. What does a young girl like you want with dark-rimmed glasses anyway?"

"I was just reading the contract, but I won't need them at the club. I'll have the pieces memorized soon, and I'll leave them off, if you like."

"I like," he said, raising his brows in appreciation of her unadorned eyes, after she had removed the glasses. "Nice big, bright eyes, with lashes a yard long. Wear lots of makeup and a low-cut gown."

"How low-cut?" she asked warily.

"You see that waitress?" he asked, pointing to a girl in a French peasant blouse and long skirt.

"Yes," she said, looking at the girl in a dark corner, filing her nails and smoking a cigarette before the club opened. She saw that the blouse generously revealed her well-rounded curves.

"That's the idea. Sexy, but refined," Jerry added, smiling at the refinement of filing nails in public. "Your playing's all right, better than Aimée's, but you have to look right for the part too. I get a lot of single nobs here. They're travelers, some of them. They want a pretty face to look at to forget the ugly wife at home. Let 'em look, but that's all. They'll try to pick you up. Don't let them. I'm not running that kind of a joint. This is a high-class place. Act respectable."

"I'll try not to disgrace you, Mr. Holmes," she said, swallowing a grin.

"Call me Jerry. We're friendly-like here. Just one big happy family."

He cast a cautious eye toward one important member of the family—his wife. Vera Holmes examined Laura closely and liked what she saw. A

nice, decent girl, she thought, not a trollop like that
Aimée. Vera sauntered over to the organ. She was a
plump matron of fifty-odd years, who passed for a
decade younger in the dark lighting of the club.
There she tended the till, also dressed up like a
French peasant—but one with a taste for finery as
the strings of cheap beads and rings sparkling on her
neck and fingers attested. Vera was as English as her
spouse. The name Chez Nous was used to lend the
place a touch of class, a commodity in which both
she and Jerry were keenly interested. They were not
at all socially ambitious, but a classy place could
charge more for its mutton.

"How old are you, dearie?" Vera asked. "We
don't want to get in trouble with the law, hiring a
minor," she added to her husband.

"I'm of legal age. Twenty-one," Laura answered.

"You look younger," Vera persisted.

"I have my driver's license here," Laura said,
rifling her capacious bag for it. It was examined
suspiciously and returned to her.

"She'll look older with her hair fixed up. Don't
wear it clutched into a tail behind like that," Jerry
said. "With a nice gown . . ."

"Don't cheapen her, you great oaf. She's got
class," Vera told him. "Wear a fashionable evening
gown. You'll know better what to wear than we
could tell you. We don't want anything cheap or
gaudy—but not nunnish neither. You know what I
mean?"

"Red satin, or . . ." Jerry began, and was
summarily told to shut up.

"I get the idea," Laura answered, wondering just
which discreetly vulgar gown would suit them both.

"All right. The job's nine to twelve thirty," Vera said, taking over the instructions. "You play four half-hour sets with half-hour breaks between, Wednesday to Saturday. We're closed Mondays, because Monday is slow, and Tuesday isn't busy enough to hire music. On Wednesday things start to pick up. You get a salary and anything the gents want to tip. Aimée always kept a brandy snifter on her organ. She used to stick a pound note in it herself before she started to play, to show the men she didn't want loose change. They'll often put in a quid when they make a request, to impress their girl or you. You keep it. What you do outside the place is your own affair, but we don't want any trouble in here. It gives the place a bad name. Of course I'm not saying you shouldn't have a free drink off a customer if you particularly fancy him. It does no harm to be friendly—to the regular customers in particular."

"Jerry already told me. Don't worry; I won't be trying to pick up your customers. I'm very busy."

"What do you do, outside of playing the organ, I mean?" Vera asked, but it was Jerry who listened with sharper attention.

"I'm a student at the Royal Academy of Music, but it's hard making ends meet."

"Have you got no family?" Jerry asked.

"I have a brother in town. He's the minister of St. Peter's Parish. They don't make much money."

"That's the truth," Vera corroborated. "Never order anything but a glass of the cheap house wine, and if they leave a shilling tip, the girls are lucky. But we don't get many ministers of course."

"I shouldn't think Francis has ever been in a place

like this," Laura said, her eyes traveling around the cavernous room, whose walls were covered in red and gold flocked paper with large expanses of inset mirror. There were gilt sconces holding flickering electric lights that resembled candles. Real candles were on the tables. There was white linen napery and a nod to the French name in the menu, whose selections were in French with English translations.

"If you get hungry, you can have a bite in the kitchen between sets," Vera told her, feeling a streak of maternal concern for the young woman. She was slender and pale, but best of all, she wasn't forward. A forward organist was the bane of Vera's life. The one before Aimée was worse, rolling her eyes at Jerry, and he fool enough to be lending the hussy money above and beyond her salary, which was already too high. What were they in business for anyway, to support an organist or to save up and buy a poultry farm?

"Is there any quiet place I could study between sets?" Laura asked. "We have essays to do at the Academy."

"There's a wee cubbyhole in the hall next to the loo. I fancy you could use the dressing table for a desk in a pinch," Vera advised.

It had been three months now since Laura had started there. As she stood looking out at the mist, it was early April. It had been an interesting three months. She had learned how to handle the various types of wolves to which she was exposed. She was friendly, but no more, and gave out neither her last name nor her address. She occasionally joined one of the regular customers for a drink between sets but never allowed any of them to accompany her home. Jerry and Vera had taken a personal interest in her, when they learned she was innocent of such vices as soliciting their customers, helping herself to free drinks at the bar, or running home with steaks or silverware hidden under her coat. "A real nice girl" was their final assessment of her character.

They even helped her find a flat of her own after her brother's wife had given birth to a child in February. Jerry owned a row of flats two blocks behind his restaurant. It wasn't prime real estate, but it wasn't quite a slum either. With housing so scarce and so expensive, Laura was delighted to accept it. It came furnished—unfortunately in a style that suited Vera's notions of class.

"I decorated them all by myself," Mrs. Holmes said proudly when she first took Laura to examine her new home. A bright panoply of reds, oranges, yellows, and greens struck the eye most forcibly. A scarlet plush sofa sat cheek by jowl with a green upholstered chair on a yellow shaggy carpet. At the high, narrow window scarlet drapes hung stiffly. Cheap Formica tables and garish swag lamps on gilt chains completed the decor of the living room. There was a closet-sized bedroom and an even smaller kitchen with its own refrigerator and stove. Most important of all for Laura, the price was right.

"I decorated it all myself," Vera repeated as she looked around the room. "Why should I pay a decorator for, when I've got an eye in my own head as good as any of them? They were going to charge me a fortune just to pick out rugs and curtains that hang in the shops, ready to take home."

"How very nice and cheery," Laura said, quickly

examining the place for possible revision. "Would it be all right if I put in some of my own things as well? Mom left me a few bits and pieces that Francis has kept for me at his place. I'd like to have them around me. They have sentimental value," she added, so no offense would be taken.

"Why not, dear? It's your own digs, to do with as you like—so long as you don't get white rings on the tabletops, or cigarette burns in the carpet. But you don't smoke, and I know you're not the sort will be throwing wild parties."

"Of course not."

"There's plenty of your neighbors as will. That pair of women next door to you are no more models than I am, and that's a fact. They pulled the wool over Jerry's eyes and there's nothing we can do now until their lease runs out. One of them calls herself a hostess at a private gentlemen's club. There's another name for her sort, but I won't let it cross my lips. You'll not have anything to do with the likes of them, being away all day and working four nights out of the seven. I expect you visit your brother from time to time as well?"

"I'll go to him on Sunday, and of course I have my schoolwork to keep up on my free nights."

"Don't you have any beaux at all, dear? I'd think a fine-looking young girl like yourself would have rafts of them."

"I go out once in a while. Most of the kids don't have much money to spend on dates. We go to movies or lectures, and the concerts when we can get standing room."

"You'll soon be rich and famous, as soon as you're graduated. I look forward to hearing you perform at the Albert Hall. You'll look just grand in a fashionable gown. As classy as a princess."

"I hope so. I'll bring you and Jerry tickets for my debut."

"That'll be lovely. We look forward to it."

Laura did her best with the gaudy flat. Her small Persian rug concealed some part of the shag rug beneath, and a homemade afghan was placed over the sofa. Satin pillows were stored away on the top of the closet shelf, as were all the rather startling ornaments. She displayed her mother's silver tea service on a tea trolley, in lieu of a chrome freestanding ashtray from the Chez Nous. The wall ornaments, a tiger and an Oriental bird painted on black velvet, were put beneath the bed and replaced by nineteenth-century landscapes that had belonged to her mother. The large items were just too expensive to replace, so she learned to live with them. The place was far from beautiful, but at least it was less hideous than when she took possession.

Laura cast one last look at the smiling facsimile of herself in the club window, and entered the Chez Nous to prepare for her first weekly stint at the organ. Wednesday was usually the least busy of her nights, and tonight was no exception. The room was hardly more than half full when she went to her dressing room to prepare. She wore her hair brushed back from her face, so it hung over her shoulders in soft, natural waves.

Till she applied her makeup, she looked younger than her twenty-one years. She took a black pencil and drew feathery strokes across her brows, then a line all around the eye, top and bottom, with little wings at the outer ends. She carefully smudged a blue-purple cream on her eyelids and stood back. At this point in the process she looked eerily like a ghost with painted eyes. Next she applied rouge, then lipstick. She fastened on the costume earrings, great dangly things that looked like diamonds in the dim light of the dining room, but were actually rhinestones. Jerry liked her to sparkle. She slid a paste-stone sapphire ring onto her left hand. She had beautiful hands, long and slender, with shapely nails. To display them to advantage at work, she had begun using nail polish and allowed the fingernails to grow a little longer than before.

The midnight blue gown she wore was dramatic, if not as low cut as Jerry would have liked. It was scooped out in front below the collarbone and fitted neatly over her small waist and slender hips. The long sleeves that came down to her wrists lent it an air of sophistication. She was lucky in buying clothes. Her small size was often plentiful and could be bought at half price during sales. This way she could get the quality she wanted at a price she could afford—though not always during the season she wanted.

Surveying herself in the mirror, she thought that if her mother and father could see her rigged out like this, they'd think she'd become a fallen woman. But Francis had become her moral adviser, and he didn't disapprove of her work. In fact Mavis, his wife, had helped her select the four evening gowns for the job and taken in two of them for her. Francis was broad-minded enough to see nothing immoral in his Sunday organist playing at a dinner club during the week. He wasn't an old-fashioned sort of minister, out of touch with the times. He even took Mavis to the Chez Nous one evening to watch Laura perform. Like many younger clerics, he had abandoned his clerical collar and black suit when doing general parish work.

"I'm sorry I couldn't help you financially, Laurie," he said, "but with the baby coming along . . ."

"You did help, Francis. You helped a lot, letting me stay with you and Mavis for two years. I know my way around London now. It's only for one more year. I could even finish without the job, but I wanted to be able to put something aside. You know I want to try my hand at composing after I graduate."

"By then Mavis and I may have moved up to a big enough house for you to stay with us."

"Sure, or maybe I'll be married. Who knows?"

"Not to any of those fellows you meet at the club, I hope!"

"Not likely!" she replied, laughing.

There was, however, one regular customer who had proposed marriage to her. He proposed several times a week. He was always there on Wednesdays and Thursdays and sometimes on Fridays, too, but not usually on Saturday nights. She thought perhaps he went home on the weekends. Peeping around the curtain on that Wednesday night, she saw he was at his usual table.

The spotlight beamed. Jerry, in poorly cut evening clothes, announced her, and she walked to the organ with a bow and a smile to the audience. She had previously worked out her repertoire with the Holmes's. She began with a series of lively show tunes from *Mame, Hello, Dolly!, Cabaret,* and others. Their execution was easy after the more complicated works performed at the Academy. She had a bright, lively style she used for the club with many arpeggios, chromatic descents, and other flashy tricks that made the listeners think that what they were hearing was great stuff. She personally didn't consider it music, but something less worthy —show business. From long repetition she could play the pieces without sheet music, without her glasses . . . almost without thinking. This left her free to glance around at the diners and drinkers. She received a few requests and a few folded bills in her brandy snifter.

At the end of the first set she arose, bowed, and glided off behind the curtain. There she saw her suitor, waiting for her, but she was becoming concerned at his persistence and refused to spend every intermission with him. But by the end of her ten-thirty set, she'd begun to feel sorry for Sean Bowden. He rose from his table and went to the organ, to invite her for a drink before she could disappear on him again.

"Maybe at the end of the next set, Sean," she answered.

"I won't be here for the next set. I have to leave early tonight," he told her, his eyes wearing the adoring, begging aspect of a puppy. "I won't be back here for a whole week. I had hoped to talk to you before I go home. It's spring break, you know," he pointed out.

Sean was a university student, attending the London School of Economics much against his will. What he really craved was a glamorous life in one of the arts—either legitimate theater, the cinema, music, or the literary world would have suited his taste, he told her. That he had no talent in any of these directions was unfortunate.

Wishing to maintain complete privacy, Laura had never told him that she, too, was a student. She thought her air of mystery was really what had attracted him to her. He was young and romantic enough for that.

"In that case, we must have a farewell drink," she answered, going with him to his table.

"The usual?" he asked with an intimate smile, then flushed in annoyance when he knocked over a glass as he sat down. Luckily it was empty. Sean knocked things over a lot. She thought he was enduring the last months of his awkward age, or maybe he was only nervous with her. It was her role to remain oblivious to all the spilt drinks, stumbles, and stepped-on toes.

"The usual," she agreed.

When with Sean, her *usual* was a glass of red house-wine, chosen because it was the cheapest thing on the menu. Since he was a student, she felt he was likely to be overburdening his wallet already coming here so often. He never ordered a meal but came in late and had a drink. There was no actual air of poverty about him. He was well-dressed but casual. Tonight he wore a tweed sport jacket with a cashmere sweater beneath it. Sean was tall but adolescent, just emerging from the period when his legs were too long and body too thin. In a few years he'd be exceedingly handsome, but at the moment he was gauche with his dark brown hair falling over his forehead, and a pair of brown eyes gazing at her as though she were a vision from heaven. Nearly as much as he wanted Laura, he wanted to be a suave, sophisticated man-about-town.

When their drinks were on the table, he reached tentatively for her fingers, narrowly missing a vase containing one white rose. "I'll be gone all week," he said, looking to see how this news struck her.

She concealed her immense relief with a sad little smile. "I suppose you're going home?" she asked.

"Yes, to Hazelhurst, my family home, you know, in Sussex."

"That'll be a nice holiday for you."

"It won't be nice, so far from you," he answered, squeezing her fingers. "If it weren't that my father is ill, I wouldn't go at all."

She gently extracted the fingers on the pretext of taking a sip of her wine. A sip was all she took, as the single drink was to be stretched over the half hour of their visit.

"What will you do while I'm away?" he asked.

"I'll be here Wednesday through Saturday, pounding the organ," she told him.

"Pounding? You play like an angel. You *look* like an angel, with your hair spun fine as silver about your shoulders. I wish you'd tell me all about yourself, Laura."

"There isn't much to tell."

"You should live in an enchanted castle with a fairy godmother. You should dine on nectar and read poetry all day long."

"How very tedious. I shouldn't like that at all. I have no exotic tastes or background, Sean. I am not a princess or a spy or a young widow, as you have suggested in the past. I'm just a plain, average English girl, working for a living."

"Don't disillusion me. There isn't a plain, average bone in your entire body," he contradicted enthusiastically. "Your bones are wrought of ivory filigree or crystal. I wish you'd come home to Hazelhurst with me and let me introduce you to my family."

"Dear Sean," she said in a maternal way, patting his hand, "what would be the point of it? We're just friends, and that is all we'll ever be. I'm flattered that you like me so much, but . . ."

"*Like* you?" he rejoined, offended. "I've told you a hundred times I adore you, I worship you. I look forward all day to the evening, when I can come and look at you. I spend the evenings when you aren't here walking the streets, looking in the throng for a glimpse of you, hoping I might see you, follow you home, and learn who you are."

"You'd be much better employed studying," she scolded. "How did you do in your exams?"

"Results aren't posted yet. I probably failed miserably. How can I expect to be interested in mergers and inflation and interest rates, when all I want to do is be with you? I wish you'd marry me, Laura, and let me take you away from this." One slender hand was waved in a semicircle around the room. It missed a passing tray of glasses by a hair's breadth and hit a waiter's elbow. Sean gave the man an offended look and resumed his lovemaking. "You're out of place here, like a fragile and delicate orchid blooming in a rubbish heap."

"How can you say so? This is a classy joint," she teased.

"I little thought when I came here two months ago how it would change my life," he mused. "I came with another girl; imagine! I haven't been out with anyone since that fateful evening."

"You should go out with some nice girl your own age."

"There's not that much difference in our ages. I'm not a teenager, after all," he boasted with the eagerness of one who was not much beyond his teens. "I could quit university and take a job."

"Oh, Sean! Really, you make me very angry when you talk like that. Think of your future!"

"I can't bear to think of a future without *you!*" he answered ardently.

"You have to finish your education. This isn't the time for you to be imagining you're in love with me, a woman you don't even know except by sight."

"Why won't you tell me about yourself? You know all about me. It's not fair."

"I told you the first time I agreed to have a drink with you that I never tell my name or address or phone number to customers. You accepted my friendship on those terms. If you want to stop coming, I won't be offended. It would be better if you *didn't* come here anymore."

"Why are you being so cruel to me, especially now when I have to be away for a week? I won't have a moment's peace worrying about it. I don't think I'll go home after all. Of course if I don't, my mother will have a fit, and my brother will probably have the police out chasing me. They treat me as though I were a child," he said with a childish sulk. Reaching for his glass, his hand collided with the vase of flowers and knocked it over. "I don't know why they don't have decent-sized tables here," he scolded.

"In a way you are a child," she told him, to try to shock him into sane behavior. "If I were a different sort of woman, I could take advantage of you."

"I know you'd never do that. You won't even let me take you home or send you flowers. Is there . . . is there another man? Is that it?" he asked fearfully.

She considered telling him there was, to stop his foolish dangling after her, but in the end thought he might create an unpleasant scene. "No, Sean, I'm just not interested in men at this point in my life."

"You have been badly used by them! That's it. Did he beat you?" he asked, eyes flashing, hands clenching into fists to avenge her cruel treatment.

"No, nobody beat me. Don't be so melodramatic."

"There must be some reason you're so elusive. You're like a beautiful hummingbird, always hovering just beyond my grasp. I have never told you this, Laura, but if you thought I couldn't provide for you, it's not true. My family is quite wealthy. I personally have some fortune from an uncle—will have it in my own control, I mean, when I'm of age—that is, it is tied up in a stupid trust fund, but it is my own money."

"So you think I'm a gold digger!" she charged, using any pretext to pick a fight with him and cool his ardor.

"No, I think you're an angel."

"You're determined to make me wear wings one way or another."

"I know money would hold no interest for you beyond providing a decent home," he said, rummaging in his inner jacket pocket. She watched with interest, curious to see what would come out. It was a small square object, dark in color. After a moment's fumbling he got the lid open and handed the box to her. She didn't accept it but sat staring at a very large diamond, or possibly rhinestone, ring, roughly the size of the costume jewelry she wore on her finger.

"It's a family heirloom," he said simply. He lifted the ring out and reached for her fingers.

Curious to determine if the thing were real, she let him slide it on her finger and examined it. It was an antique setting, severely elegant in the Tiffany style, with prongs holding the monstrous diamond in place.

"Where did you get this, Sean? It's *beautiful!*" she exclaimed.

"Not nearly so beautiful as you. Will you accept it? It's an engagement ring," he added hastily.

"No, of course I won't," she said, removing it and handing it back to him.

"It's been in my family for generations. My great-uncle Thaddeus was in India in the early 1800's and brought the stone back. Please wear it. I'd like to have this business settled before I leave town."

"It *is* settled!" she said, with one last lingering glance of admiration at the ring.

But in Sean's mind, it would be far from settled until he got the diamond on her finger. The half hour dragged on, with Sean pleading with her to marry him, while she parried his thrusts.

"I suppose I'd better leave now," he said with a weary sigh when the time was up. "I promised my mother I'd be home this evening."

"You had better get started then."

"Yes, the train leaves in a quarter of an hour."

"Sean! You'll never make it to the station in time."

"I have a cab that's waiting. *Promise* me you'll still be here when I come back."

"I have no intention of quitting my job. I'll be here, God willing."

He kissed her fingers and left the table.

But when she got to the organ, she saw he was still standing at the doorway watching her and very likely missing his train. Finally he left.

"Your beau left early tonight," Vera said, when she went to the kitchen for a cup of coffee after the third set.

"Yes, he's going home for the holiday, thank goodness. He's becoming awfully persistent. I wish I could get rid of him. He actually offered me a diamond tonight."

"You never mean it! You're too soft-hearted. The thing to do is to sit with someone else for a few nights, and he'll take the hint."

"I didn't even acknowledge his presence for one whole week, but he just kept coming, wearing his hang-dog expression till I couldn't stand it any longer."

"He's not a bad-looking fellow," Vera pointed out. "Rich, too, to judge by his jackets. Was it a big diamond?"

"A whopper. I wonder where he got it. He said it was a family heirloom."

"Well, he couldn't come here night after night if he was a pauper. We have our cover charge. We don't get many students at all. Bowden, did you say the name is?"

"Yes, Sean Bowden."

"I've heard that name before somewhere. Read it in the papers, I think, or heard it on the telly. What does his father do?"

"He seems to live out of town. I've never asked him. He usually talks about 'us.'"

"It might be worth your while to find out, Laura. Why, he could be a 'Sir' or a lord, for all we know."

"The term will soon be over. I expect he'll go home to Sussex for the summer, and that'll be the end of it."

"He is a bit young," Vera said. "Care to try a French pastry, dear? There's two plates left over, and Jerry doesn't serve them day-old. The cream goes off and makes the pastry soggy. Have a cream puff, do."

"If that's a spare lobster tail over there, I'll have that instead, if you don't mind."

"Help yourself. I don't know how Christian people can eat those nasty things, let alone pay a fortune for them," Vera said, reaching for a puff pastry.

"I won't tell you how good it is then. I want all the spare ones for myself," Laura replied, cracking the tail open and extracting the meat with a fork.

When she was finished, it was time for her final set. Jerry liked a good rousing close. They had chosen Latin music, a medley of rhumbas, several Brazilian bossa nova hits from the late sixties, with "Tico Tico" for the grand finale. This number always brought a strong round of applause. As soon as she had made her bows, she walked off the stage to leave quietly by the back door where a hired cab was waiting for her. Her gratuities permitted that extravagance, which was as much for safety as convenience.

As she was being driven home, she thought back on the evening. She'd told Sean he was lucky she wasn't the sort of woman to take advantage of him, but she knew *she* was lucky too. Had it been a wilier, more aggressive type of man who had become infatuated with her, he'd have found out before now where she lived and would be pestering her at her apartment.

Sean was so innocent and naive and so very much in love with her, she found it hard to be as firm with him as she should. When he came back, she'd tell him frankly she didn't want him to come to the club anymore. It was foolish to have him there, moping night after night. And now to be trying to give her a diamond engagement ring! Offering a valuable family heirloom to a woman whose last name he didn't even know was the height of stupidity. The boy needed a keeper. He'd be grossly offended when she sent him packing, but he'd get over it in a week or so, and they'd both be better off. She felt better, easier in her mind, after making the decision.

Chapter Two

Thursday and Friday evenings Sean was not there, which was a vast relief. On Friday the place was busy; the tips were good, and there was only one more night of performing before she would have her treasured three nights to herself.

Saturday was the big night at the Chez Nous. On Saturday she wore the best and sexiest gown. Mavis and Jerry agreed with her that the slinky black gown slit up past the knee was very dashing. In front, it was similar in cut to the blue gown but in back it dipped below her waist. She wore an extravagant-looking pair of sparkly earrings, and on the front of the dress she pinned a large pink rose just at the hip. When she wore this outfit, she was invariably greeted with a loud round of applause as soon as she appeared. The brandy snifter was always full before the night was over too.

This Saturday was no exception. The clapping was loud. She bowed and smiled and walked to the organ, her nyloned legs bringing another round of applause as the slit skirt frisked about her knees. She made a curtsy in acknowledgment of it, smiling brightly. She had long since lost her embarrassment at public performing. She enjoyed giving the audience pleasure, and if her appearance added to it, there was no harm done.

She went into her show tunes, her fingers flying over the keys, the rhinestone ring casting prisms of dancing light. She glanced around to see if there were any celebrities in the throng. Occasionally a TV or movie star or a politician came in on a Saturday. She didn't see anyone famous that night. She noticed the table for two closest to her organ was empty, which was peculiar on a Saturday. They usually had to turn people away. Midway through her first set, a man was led to the table by the waiter, indicating he had made a reservation. He was alone, which was not unusual. Traveling businessmen often came in alone, and left alone too. If they came in hopes of picking up a girl, they were disappointed. Jerry was serious about running a classy joint.

She noticed from the corner of her eye that this one was handsome. He was tall with dark hair and eyes, rather Latin-looking, she thought. Many of the customers had finished dinner and were drinking, but the man ordered a full dinner and settled back with a glass of wine to wait for it. While he sipped, he looked at the organist with interest on his rather swarthy face. She knew that before the evening was over, he would invite her to join him for a drink. He was exactly the sort of customer she avoided—an older, experienced man of the world. He had a predatory, sensuous face and eyes that spoke volumes. After exchanging a few unintentional glances, she was careful not to look at him again, as his eyes seemed to have settled firmly on her. He clapped lazily at the end of each selection.

She finished the first set with no spoken communication from him. When she went to the organ for her next set, he rose and lounged toward her.

"Bon soir, mam'selle," he said with a graceful bow and a smile. "Do you take requests?" His voice was low and attractive with a faint accent.

"Yes, if I know the tune you like," she answered, feeling unaccountably nervous, but soon deciding it was his manner that explained it. His eyes wandered over her lips, her neck, and her bosom in quite open admiration. She held his French nationality accountable for it and congratulated herself at having pegged him correctly.

"Are you familiar with 'La Vie en Rose'?" he asked.

"I know it. Would you like me to play it for you?"

"I would be charmed. Do you also sing?"

"No, I don't. It's an Edith Piaf song, isn't it?"

"Yes. She was one of the best chanteuses of the century, or so we in France believe. 'The Little Sparrow,' we called her. *You* we would have to name a dove. You do not sing, but your voice has the gentle cooing quality of the dove."

"You're from France, are you?" she asked, feeling the question stupid, as he had just said so.

"Paris," he replied, giving it the French pronunciation. He folded a bill into her brandy snifter as he spoke. She knew by the color that it was a five pound note, which displeased her, as it was much too much

for only playing a request. He obviously was expecting more than that for his money.

She played the song with a nod to him at its end. He clapped lazily as before and nodded back with a smile. He had finished his dinner and studied the dessert menu. While she played, a dessert was flambéed at his table. He ate with only an occasional glance at her. She was happy the second set finished without his accosting her. She had a request to join another customer for a drink and declined in a voice loud enough for him to hear, so he'd take the hint that she didn't fraternize with customers. She made the mistake of looking to determine if he had in fact heard and saw him smiling softly at her. He lifted his brows and nodded his head approvingly. But somehow there was more than approval in those black eyes; there was anticipation. He thought she was waiting for *him* to ask her! Flustered, she arose and bolted from the room in unseemly haste, wishing he'd be gone by the time she returned. But he was still there, nursing a brandy.

Before she began to play, he rose and came toward her. "May I buy you a drink, mam'selle?" he asked very politely. "It is hard work, first entertaining the gentlemen, then having to discourage them."

"You have already been too generous. I don't drink while I am playing. Thank you."

"Afterward, you will join me at my table? The *bourgeois gentilhomme* who prevented us before has now taken his departure."

"I don't think so. Thank you for asking me," she said, looking at the keyboard, inviting him to leave without saying it.

"But I thought . . . please," he said in a soft,

coaxing voice. "I am alone in town, a stranger. I want only to share a few moments of conversation with you. Won't you oblige me?"

"All right," she said on impulse. She didn't look too closely into her motives, telling herself that he wasn't a Londoner and couldn't become a pest like Sean. The next intermission was the last one of the evening. After her fourth set she could hop into her taxi and go straight home. There could be no harm in it, and really he was very handsome.

When the set was over, he stood up to accompany her to his table. "I did not know what mam'selle likes to drink. A cognac, champagne . . . ?"

"I usually have red wine," she told him. "The waiter knows."

"You must allow me to recommend something. We French all consider ourselves experts on wine. You prefer a Bordeaux, Médoc . . . or something lighter? A Beaujolais perhaps, Chinon?" He stopped and looked at her expectantly.

"Just the house wine, if you please."

"That I forbid, *absolument*. It will give you a very poor opinion of our vineyards. Mam'selle shall have a light red wine, a Beaujolais, I think. Hmm, we do not have an adequate choice," he ran on, frowning at the wine list. "I shall speak to the *sommelier*."

"You mustn't bother. In fact, we don't have a wine steward here. I always just have the house wine."

"Which tells me mam'selle does not receive a commission on the drinks she induces her . . . friends to purchase on her behalf," he said, but with a playful air that made it impossible to take offense. "No matter, we shall have a decent bottle all the same." He ordered a bottle whose astronomical price was well known to Laura.

"I don't know that much about wine. I won't appreciate it. And really, a whole bottle . . ." she protested vainly.

"I shall help you to imbibe it. This is proper English, *imbibe?*"

"Yes, a little formal. More usually we say *drink.*"

"I shall remember it."

"You speak very good English, Mr. . . ."

"Dufresne," he said, bowing his head. "Henri Dufresne. I believe I have the honor to address the 'Lovely Laura.' It was your picture in the front that drew me to this place. That and its name, which is most misleading. It is not at all a French restaurant, as I had hoped."

"Only the name is French," she agreed with a rueful smile.

"The picture also was misleading. It does not begin to do 'Lovely Laura' justice," he said, his dark eyes examining her closely. She felt an involuntary blush.

"Thank you," she said quietly.

"It is my firm belief you should sue the cartoonist who displayed such a gross caricature of your appearance. May I know your family name?"

"I don't tell—that is, call me Jones. Laura Jones." Somehow it was impossible to tell this suave foreigner that she wouldn't tell him her name. It seemed too childish.

The waiter brought the wine, showed Dufresne the label, at which he peered with interest, then poured a taste into a glass. The Frenchman rolled it around his tongue judiciously with first a slight grimace, but then a nod of acceptance. "It will do. Beaujolais should be served warmer, never cooler than 10 degrees centigrade, preferably 12. The cork also is too short, but it is not, alas, one of the great wines. It is to be expected. It is the best I can do, Mam'selle Jones," he apologized.

"It'll be fine," she assured him. Certainly it was much better than the house wine she usually accepted.

"You seem to know a good deal about wines," she said, to make light conversation.

"Wine and women—all Frenchmen know these two subjects thoroughly. May I say, the women Chez Nous are of a much higher quality than the wines. More expensive, too, I imagine," he added, with a little questioning smile.

Her heart sank. He was being even more frank about his intentions than she had feared. "The women are not for sale at any price, Monsieur. If you are looking for *that* sort of company . . ."

"Please? I have offended?" he asked, frowning in consternation. "I did not mean harm. Ah, you thought I referred to buying a lady's favors, no? That was not my meaning."

She could think of no other construction that could be placed on his words but was eager to quit the topic. "Perhaps your English is not as good as I thought," she said.

"I have taught it to myself. I go very often to the English movies and read their abominable books and journals. I also come to England many times on business."

"What business are you in, Mr. Dufresne?" she asked, trying to hit on a harmless topic.

"Many businesses. I have a partnership in a

vineyard in the Rhone Valley, also a hotel nearby. Presently I am in London meeting with gentlemen of the movie industry."

"Are you going to make a film about your vineyard?" she asked, thinking it was some sort of advertisement for his company.

"Not at all. It is an entertainment film, a movie. It will be shot in London mostly with some scenes in Paris. It is not the *Tale of Two Cities*, however, though I adore your Charles Dickens. No, it is a modern film with very much intrigue and love."

"You're a movie producer, you mean?" she asked, smiling in surprise at having actually met one of these fabled gentlemen.

"I am financing it only. I do not take an active part in its direction and so on, as this will be my first venture in the cinema. I shall help to select the cast, however. Do you do any acting, Laura?"

"No, no. I've never acted," she told him.

"But you are so very beautiful! As soon as I saw how lovely is Laura, not at all like her picture outside, I changed Maria's raven hair to silver blond, like the moonlight. Maria is our heroine in the movie. It is an unusual shade you have tinted your hair."

"My hair color doesn't come out of a bottle, thank you very much!"

"How womanlike you are, Laura. Two compliments I give you, and you discover instead an insult. Allow me to apologize for my gaucherie. And you are not at all interested in acting for me?"

"It sounds fascinating, but no, I'm not interested."

"This is very strange. In Paris all the beautiful young girls will want to be a film star."

"You should have no trouble casting it then."

"Maria is an English girl."

"Many English girls would like to be a film star too."

"But not Laura?" he asked sadly.

"I'm afraid not."

"What do you do, when you are not performing magic on the organ?"

"I—I have another occupation. A daytime job," she said vaguely. Again she found it impossible to say she wouldn't discuss it. He was too worldly, too communicative of his own circumstances.

"What sort of job?" he persisted. "I come to fear mam'selle is a spy, she is so secretive of her doings."

"I give organ lessons," she said, to prevent claiming knowledge in some field of which she was ignorant.

"I see. You give these lessons at your home?"

"No, at a school," she told him.

"What school?"

"The Royal Organ Academy," she replied, trusting a foreigner wouldn't know it for an invention.

"This is affiliated with the Royal Academy of Music?" he asked.

"No, not really. They just borrowed the name," she lied, uncomfortable with his associating her with her own academy.

"You hope one day to play at Albert Hall, to tour the continent, making great music? I think your audience would welcome the variety your repertoire offers," he said in some tone that she could not quite figure out. Quite possibly he was laughing at her.

"I realize, as I am sure *you* do, that what I play here is not concert-hall caliber. This is music to eat and drink by, background music," she said, her temper rising.

"Then you are not a *serious* musician, but only an entertainer?"

"I *am* serious! I play a different type of organ than this, when I don't have to play for money, Mr. Dufresne."

"I see. My name is Henri, by the by. How late in the evening do you work here?"

"Very late. Till twelve thirty," she said, knowing from past encounters with his sort what he had in mind.

"That is not so late. There must be some other entertainments still open at that hour. Tomorrow is Sunday, the day of rest," he pointed out.

"Not for me. I also play the organ on Sunday."

"Here?"

"No . . . elsewhere."

He frowned. *"More* secrets. Is it that you have a husband?"

"Good heavens, no! I play at a church, if you must have all my secrets."

"What church?" he asked at once.

"Not St. Paul's Cathedral. A small local church. You wouldn't know of it."

"I would if you told me. Also I would find it. I am part bird—homing pigeon, to be precise. I tell you all *my* secrets."

"It's not nice to pry, Henri. It is not one of the tourist attractions of the city. You won't be missing anything."

"I will be missing *you,*" he said with a boyish frown. "You will not tell me?"

"There's no point," she replied, and looked at her watch, wishing to escape.

"I know what it is. You are tired and hungry after so much playing of the organ. Let me take you out for a late dinner."

"I don't go out with the customers. It's the policy of the place. I really must go now."

"The policy is that you may only sit with a customer in the restaurant, and not go with him outside of it?" She nodded. "That is a strange policy. I have not come across it before."

"It's the policy here," she insisted. "I have to powder my nose before my next set. Thank you for the wine. I enjoyed it."

"Not nearly so much as I enjoyed the charming company," he said, rising to make a formal bow before she left. Heads in the room turned to admire the tall man and his courtly grace.

She avoided his glances during the next set. There was something forward in Henri Dufresne that unnerved her. He asked too many questions, was too insistent. He was handsome and amusing enough, but she knew instinctively his only interest in her was sexual.

When her rousing Latin-American set was finished, she took her final bow and hastened to the kitchen. She'd have a lobster tail, if cook had made any extra, and then go home.

"Anything good to eat?" she asked Chester, the chef.

"I'm making a whole dinner for you, Laura. Escargots, broiled lobster with drawn butter, Parisienne potatoes, and a house salad. Where are you going to put all this food, eh?"

"I couldn't eat all that! Though it *does* look delicious. What happened? Did someone order and have to leave?"

"No, he's still there waiting for you, as far as I know. The Frenchie ordered it. He asked the waiter what you liked and had it prepared."

"Henri Dufresne?" she asked, feeling a spurt of anger, even apprehension, at his bold move.

"I guess that's the name. They say he's wonderfully handsome, the waitresses."

"I didn't tell him I'd join him for dinner."

"You'd better. You know what this is costing him. He's ordered champagne too—the good stuff, from France."

"He takes a lot for granted. It looks lovely, Chester, but I'm afraid Mr. Dufresne won't expect me to go home alone if I accept his hospitality."

"What he expects and what he gets are two different things. I'll drive you home afterward, if you like. We'll teach him a lesson. Eat and run. It'll serve him right, and it's a shame to waste this dinner."

After considering this suggestion a moment, she thought the lesson wouldn't do Mr. Dufresne any harm. "All right, I'll do it. Have your car ready for a fast getaway. About an hour, I'd say. Will you be through by then?"

"We're not taking any more dinner orders. I'll be ready and waiting. Enjoy your dinner," he said, and smiled conspiratorially.

Certain that she'd never have to see Dufresne again, she decided to enjoy the dinner. "You are naughty, Henri," she scolded when she went to join him. "I told you I wouldn't have dinner with you."

"*Excusez-moi,* mam'selle. You said you could not have dinner with me outside of this establishment. I understood you to mean I should order your dinner here."

"You are an unconscionable liar, Henri Dufresne. You did not think anything of the sort. You tricked me."

"It is a delicious trick, *non?*" he asked with a bold smile as the plate of escargots was placed in front of her. Chester did them in champagne with butter and spices, and they were the pride of Chez Nous. It was an expensive delicacy she seldom got to enjoy.

"Delicious," she agreed, and took up her clamp to hold the shell steady while she extracted the meat.

"I have ordered champagne. It is called Dom Perignon on the menu. I doubt it is one of the better years. Probably '53, when the mold invaded the vines."

He tasted it judiciously and made no slurs on it. Once the two glasses were poured, he waved the waiter away. "I shall pour the next glass myself, and from the proper height. We do not want a fountain after all, but prefer that a few of the bubbles remain in the liquid. I knew as soon as he wrenched the cork out so improperly that he would also destroy the pouring, but one does not like to complain."

"I have noticed you are very much averse to making a complaint," she said with an arch smile.

"Ah, you are making fun at me. Excellent! I like a woman who sparkles. Too much politeness is what one dislikes in English women, as a rule. That is not a complaint, but only an observation," he added, holding up one finger with a very Gallic air.

"Of course. And what observation have you to make on the glass itself? Don't tell me that is to escape your complimenting."

"I was not going to mention it, but a glass ought in fact to have rounded sides and be narrower, not wider, at the top, to enable us to enjoy the bouquet. It is Hollywood that is to blame for the world using improper wine glasses."

"You will use proper wine glasses in your film, of course."

"Everything about my film will be proper. The temperature of the champagne will be 7 degrees centigrade, instead of the chill your John Bull *sommelier* has used to destroy this bottle. But I do not complain!" he added swiftly, then laughed, tossing back his head. He used his hands lavishly as he spoke. His high spirits, his accent, and his whole manner amused her. She settled down to enjoy the meal and the unusual luxury of being a guest, rather than a performer.

"I wish to propose a toast. No, do not lift your glass yet. It is to you. To the loveliest lady who ever placed her fingers on the organ keys and refused to tell Henri Dufresne where she hides her organs. I warn you, mam'selle, before the bottle is empty, I shall have insulted all of your secrets out of your sealed lips. Now you may drink," he said.

"It's like drinking firecrackers!" she exclaimed as the bubbles broke against her lips.

"It has been likened before to drinking stars. Your words are less poetical but more descriptive. Have you not tasted champagne before?"

"I had it at my brother's graduation, but it wasn't so delicious. Wrong glasses, no doubt—Hollywood's fault. Or perhaps it wasn't Dom Perignon. Is this a very good kind of champagne?"

"Some think it the best, though of course the vintage is always of importance. Odd-numbered years are usually preferable to even. It is a sort of

superstition. '45, '47, '49, and so on. But '62 and '66
were exceptions. And '51 was actually a disaster.
What is mam'selle's vintage, if I dare to inquire?"

"An even year, I fear. The *exact* year of course is a
deep, dark secret, known only to the Secret Service."

"Not so old as to have to conceal your birth date,
surely! You blush; I shall be a proper gentleman and
change the subject. I am very fond of Veuve
Clicquot champagne myself, or perhaps it is only the
history of it that appeals to my romantic nature.
Veuve means widow. It was said to have been made
by the widow Clicquot to support her family when
her husband died. I promised to amuse you with
stories while you dined, so I shall tell you all about
champagne," he decided, and setting his elbows on
the table, he proceeded to do just that. While she ate
the escargots, he outlined the area of the northeast-
ern province of France that produced grapes that
merited the name of champagne, and which
travesties of wines dared to usurp the name.

While she ate and he talked, they also drank the
champagne, which went down very easily. "Do have
another glass. One of the great advantages of a good
champagne is that it does not cause any malady in
the morning. *Hangover,* I think you call it here. A
strange word, no? We call it *gueule de bois* in
France, which is even more strange. Wooden jaw,
animal jaw, the word *gueule* means. Do you think it
an accurate description?"

"I wouldn't know. I've never had a hangover,"
she replied, trying her salad.

"What—in all your years working in such a place
as this, you never once indulged in an excess of
wine?" he asked, surprised at her answer.

"I've only been here three months. I have a feeling tomorrow may teach me what the word *hangover* means."

"Do not fear it. Good champagne does not give a hangover. Good brandy does; I can attest to the fact. But in France, brandy is understood to be a permissible weakness in gentlemen, like a married man's having a mistress."

"Are you married?" she asked, wondering that this had not so much as occurred to her.

"I? No, no. You see no ring on my left hand."

She looked at his ringless fingers. "No, and no white mark where it was removed for the occasion either," she told him with a knowing smile. "Not that it proves anything. Not all married men wear wedding rings."

"*No* bachelors wear them, to my knowledge. We are falling into a categorical syllogism here. How excruciatingly dull, and I had promised to be amusing. I shall do much better over your lobster."

When this dish arrived, she was surprised to see her glass empty again. "It *does* go down very easily, doesn't it?" she asked with an apologetic smile.

"Very easily, but that is the mark of an excellent wine, you know. It is only the vinegars that catch in the gullet. The word *vinegar* means sour wine, *vin aigre.*"

"I didn't know that. I'm getting a free education while I eat."

"A second language is always an education. Do you speak any other languages than English and organ?"

"School French, a smattering of Italian. I know how to order dinner and ask for the closest hotel, that sort of thing."

"I assume then that you have been to Italy?"

"For a short holiday a few years ago. It was lovely."

"The company in which one travels makes the vacation. You must have been in good company."

"Good *proper* company, my brother."

"You would adore France, nearly as much as France would adore you. Perhaps you will come and visit me one day?"

"I shouldn't think that is very likely."

"You will not reconsider my movie? The pay is excellent, for the right woman."

"What would it pay?" she asked, out of general interest, and perhaps because the wine was going to her head.

"For the right woman?" he asked with a significant look.

"I don't imagine you will hire someone you consider the *wrong* woman for the part," she parried.

"Very true. You keep a remarkably straight head for one who does not usually drink much wine. I too keep my head straight. I remembered not to say *imbibe*. For the right woman, we are speaking of an allowance sufficiently high to allow her an elegant apartment, fine clothing, some jewelry, her own car. . . ."

"Allowance? You mean salary surely."

"It is not the same thing?" he asked with one of his confused frowns. "Payment of money was my meaning."

"Then the word you want is salary. Allowance has other connotations in England. It's usually paid to dependents—children and others. It isn't payment for work." But her stronger objection was that it was the term used for monies given to mistresses. Something in his wary regard told her he was familiar with this meaning.

"I too am having an education in this second language," he said, taking no offense. "It is interesting, the word *salary*. It comes to us from the Latin for *salt*, you know. In ancient days, salt was a valuable commodity. The Roman soldiers got their weekly ration of salt, as folks today get their ration of money. But we have digressed from the question. The actual salary for the role of Maria has not been established. It will be generous, to answer your question; are you interested at all?"

"I become less interested all the time. I'm not an actress."

"You underestimate yourself. I think you are a very good actress," he replied in a bland tone. "How is the lobster?" he added before she had time to say anything else.

"Excellent."

"The food in France is pure delight. The sauces in particular are unmatched elsewhere and of course not even attempted in England."

"I liked the food in Italy," she remarked.

"I cannot care for pasta nor for the tomato sauce flavored in the heavy Italian manner with too much of every spice. But then no other country can hope to please the palate of a Frenchman. We shall see next what your *patron* dares to call French pastry. I shall join you for coffee and liqueur, but first we must finish this champagne," he said, emptying the bottle into her glass.

"I'm sure I've had more than my share," she said, but it was only half a glass, so she accepted it.

"What does a teacher and organ player do after church on Sunday?" he asked, settling back to watch her.

"I visit my family and usually take dinner with them."

"That leaves a long day to go through. I have hired a car for the duration of my visit. I would be happy for a guide, to show me the countryside. Will you come with me?"

She sighed and shook her head. "I only agreed to have one drink with you, Henri. You tricked me into having this dinner. It was lovely; I enjoyed it and your company, but we won't be meeting again."

He looked deeply into her eyes, adopting a wistful expression. *"You* enjoyed it; *I* enjoyed it; why should we not meet again? It is so seldom one meets . . . someone like you."

"The world is full of women like me."

"Where do they hide themselves? It is a conspiracy against Henri Dufresne. Is it going to be necessary for me to prolong my visit to England indefinitely? Is it only here, Chez Nous, that I am to be allowed to meet you, Laura? April is so beautiful in Paris. You would enjoy to see the trees in bloom along the Seine, to drive in the countryside . . ."

"If that's an invitation to Paris, the answer is no. Not even no, thank you. Just no."

"I referred to my film!" he said hastily. "Always you place the wrong construction on my innocent phrases. I was not suggesting anything *déclassé.*"

"I'm sorry if I misunderstood."

"I imagine a woman like you receives many such proposals. It is to be expected, working as an entertainer, but I do not mean to offend you again.

Naturally everyone must live. Will you come with me tomorrow?"

"I can't. I'm busy."

"Then I shall return Chez Nous to hear you play again. Every night I shall be here, till 'Lovely Laura' has pity and agrees to go out with me."

"Don't waste your time and money, Henri."

"I have much money!"

"I won't be here again till . . . that is, I don't work here every night."

"Wednesday to Saturday, *n'est-ce pas?*"

"How did you know that?"

"The sign in front says so. Wednesday through Saturday, Lovely Laura entertains at the organ. She entertains much better at the table. I want to thank you for a marvelous evening, even if I didn't learn all your secrets." His hands stole across the linen to grab hers. His eyes were like two black diamonds, deep and glittering in the candlelight. "Let me take you home. Who will know that you break the rules?" he said persuasively.

"Please don't ask it of me," she answered softly. She feared that if he persisted, she'd succumb to the temptation. She knew too that the whirling in her head was due as much to this charming, handsome Frenchman as to the champagne. She looked at his sensuous lips, and wondered how it would feel to be kissed by them. She thought it would feel very exciting, very good.

"I am going to be bad again and disobey you. Please," he coaxed. His eyes settled on her lips. She could almost feel their caress.

"Excuse me. I have to powder my nose," she said, and jumped up.

She went to the powder room, then to the kitchen. "Take me home, Chester," she said.

"I'm ready. How did you like my dinner?"

"It was exquisite. The most enjoyable meal I've ever had."

"Hah, the Frenchie won't think so when he gets the bill and no girl for his trouble."

"How much is it?" she asked, feeling a qualm of conscience.

He told her the staggering sum. It seemed suddenly a horrible trick to play, especially to a guest in her country.

"I'll pay it. Don't give him the bill—for my dinner, I mean. He can pay for his own, but not mine."

"Don't be a ninny!" Chester chided.

"I'm not. He's really very nice. I don't want to play such a shabby trick on him. I'll tell Jerry."

The contents of her brandy snifter covered the meal. Saturday was payday, so she got her paycheck. It was also the day she received her free bottle of wine. Jerry got his house wine at a great discount, and it was his custom to give Laura and the chef a bottle a week to keep them in good spirits—and more practically, to keep them from asking for more money. Laura's friends appreciated it when they came to call.

She slipped out the back door into Chester's car with her bottle and was sped to her apartment. It was impossible not to think about the offer she'd just rejected. It would have been exciting to be in a movie, but there was just enough ambiguity in the offer so that she had no real thought of accepting it. He was obviously a man of the world, and quite possibly it was understood in his circle that "the right woman" was expected to act the role of mistress as well as that of Maria. Well, it had been an interesting evening in any case and an expensive one too. But she slept well, with her conscience free of having saddled him with the bill.

Chapter Three

Laura felt no traces of a hangover on Sunday morning. She rose later than on weekdays but not quite as late as she would have liked, since she had to play the organ at her brother's church. It was a lovely day, with the warm scent of spring in the air. She read the weekend paper as she sipped her coffee and saw that Hans Grebel, the Austrian organist, was performing a concert of ecclesiastical music at St. George's in Hanover Square that afternoon. There was no admission charge, though of course a collection would be taken.

After church her brother Francis invited her home for lunch. She sometimes spent the entire Sunday with his family, remaining for dinner, but with the organ recital at two thirty, she told them she didn't think she'd come back that day.

"It's a long ride away," she explained. "I'll just go home afterward and make a sandwich. I don't need another big meal after this lovely lunch."

"Suit yourself, Laura. Mavis and I are taking the baby to the park. It's too beautiful out to stay inside." Francis replied.

"It is awfully nice out, but I don't want to miss Hans Grebel. Perhaps I'll walk home after the concert. I'll call you later in the week."

She left to catch a bus to St. George's. The audience was sparse on a fine spring Sunday afternoon, but she recognized a few of her fellow students from the Academy and went to sit with them. The rest of the audience were elderly people for the most part, wanting a quiet place to rest and some not overly strenuous entertainment. A few of them dozed off, their heads nodding against their shoulders or chests. Grebel played well. The organ swelled to the strains of *Ave Maria*. It was the version from Bach's C-major Prelude, done by Gounod. Her first concern was to figure out the setting Grebel was using: eight-foot strings and clarinet on the upper board, melodia on the lower. Soon her mind was wandering.

It was fitting that Grebel, an Austrian, should choose Bach for his opening number, she thought. Interesting too that Gounod, a Frenchman, should have based his *Ave Maria* on Bach's work. And here it was, being appreciated years later by an English audience. Music was an international language, transcending national and geographical boundaries. Though the organ no longer enjoyed its former popularity, it had survived since the third century B.C., when the Greek engineer developed his hydraulis, the first organ, using water to compress the air. It had survived the Dark and the Middle Ages and Laura had no doubt that it would go on surviving in its new electronic form.

She was wafted away on a cloud of mysticism and symbolism as the music rolled around her. The High Baroque was her favorite period. Who could remain unmoved by the magical, celestial sounds, calling from the depths of the soul to those secret corners of consciousness where some intimations of immortality crouched? This was the proper setting to appreciate the organ, and she remembered with a twinge of something very like guilt the base use to which it was put at the dinner club where she worked. But it was only a means to an end. One day she hoped to play this superb music as well as Hans Grebel played, extracting every ounce of emotion from it to thrill her audience.

It wouldn't be an easy life. Here was Hans, one of the better organists in the Western world, playing to only a handful of listeners, half of them snoozing. She'd never be rich. Even if she succeeded in composing organ music, there wouldn't be much money in it, quite possibly not even a decent living. She'd probably have to teach and play for weddings besides to make ends meet. Yet she had no thought of abandoning her work. She deposited her few coins when the plate was passed and left with her friends.

"I'm going up to the choir to meet Hans Grebel," one of the students said. "I'd like to see him, and he might appreciate it to know a few people really enjoyed his music. Not many here, huh?"

They surveyed the audience, noticing the number of empty seats. "Who's that man?" her friend asked, tossing her head to the back of the assembly. "Handsome!"

Looking in the direction indicated, Laura saw the unmistakable outline of Henri Dufresne. Her first reaction was a sense of elation, followed rather quickly by a desire to escape, after having ducked out on him the night before. He'd already seen her though, and was taking a tentative step toward her.

"Do you know him?" her friend asked, incredulous.

"Yes, he's sort of a friend of mine."

"Lucky you!"

"I wasn't sure it was you," he said, bowing with a side glance to take in her friends.

She felt she should make introductions, but in a church it was possible to refrain. As they approached the rear door, her friends waved good-bye and went up to the choir loft.

"It's me, all right," she answered. He was smiling, apparently having forgiven her behavior of the night before.

"You look so different!"

"In what way? Oh, you mean I'm not wearing my stage makeup. I hope you didn't think I played the church organ in an evening gown, with a pound of paint on my face and several pounds of rhinestones on my fingers and ears."

"Not only the makeup—the costume—everything. You look so . . . young."

"I'm not quite ancient yet. How old did you take me for?"

"Twenty-eight, thirty, or thereabouts." She smiled at having appeared so mature and sophisticated. "You must be very young indeed to be flattered at that!" he exclaimed, smiling.

"Age is relative," she said with a careless shrug.

"But how old *are* you?" he asked bluntly as they passed from the vestibule into the bright sunshine, where her youth was even more clearly evident. Her simple, well-cut suit also looked very different from her black gown.

"I'm old enough to vote," she assured him.

"Barely, I think."

"Curious, our meeting here," she said with a questioning look, for it was so curious as to be downright improbable.

"I confess, it is not a coincidence. When you were not at any of the several churches I visited this morning, I thought you had played a joke on me. I did not think the other Laura the sort to be playing hymns, to tell the truth. But you have so many churches in London that it was still possible you spoke the truth. I gave you one last chance. If she is truly a church organist, I said to myself, after a careful study of your entertainment pages, she will go to hear Hans Grebel. I was by no means sure it was you. The hair looked the same, but I did not think 'Lovely Laura' would be with those young girls. You all looked like students, so serious and attentive. I did not hear a thing past the first bar of Gounod's *Ave Maria,* from looking and wondering. Interesting, is it not, that a French composer was chosen to open an Austrian's concert in England?"

She was struck by his having had a thought so similar to her own but remarked on another aspect of his speech. "Interesting too that M. Gounod borrowed Bach's *Prelude* for his work. Are all you Frenchmen so lacking in originality?"

"Not at all," he answered, but there was a surprised look on his face. They discussed the music for a moment. Laura had the strange idea she was being tested to see if she had done her homework.

"Do I pass?" she asked, when he stopped.

"Please forgive me. I am covered with shame for my bad manners, but when I have the good luck to encounter an expert in any field, it is my custom to ask questions and learn what I can. Obviously you know a great deal about music. You forgive me?"

"If you'll forgive me for leaving without saying good-bye last night," she bartered.

"Or at least *au revoir*," he said, smiling. "I took it as a great compliment. I concluded you were frightened of the big, bad French wolf. I was flattered that you thought me so dangerous."

"I didn't think that!"

"*Non?* Do you usually run from perfectly harmless men, who want only to buy you dinner and tell you that you are beautiful?"

"I don't usually even *meet* such gallant specimens, Henri." They had reached the end of the church sidewalk that led to the street. "Which way are you going?" she asked.

"That depends entirely on you. If you go east, I go east. If you go west, I go west. If you go straight up or straight down, I too follow that direction." He spoke with a slight accent and just enough unusual placement of his words to be interesting without being at all incomprehensible.

"I'm glad you're not angry about last night."

"Only angry that you paid for your own dinner. That will take me a while to forgive. If you let me buy you a very extravagant meal this evening, I might find it in my heart to pardon you." He said this with a gallant smile, but a curiously intent look in his eye.

She considered his suggestion. She had no real plans for the remainder of the day. The weather was beautiful, and Henri seemed less dangerous outside a church in broad daylight than he had in the shadows of Chez Nous, plying her with champagne. He was a stranger in her country; it seemed almost un-Christian to desert him, leaving him to get through the afternoon and evening alone.

"Don't you have anything else to do? No plans at all?"

"I know no one in London."

"What of your business contacts, the men you are making the movie with?"

"Ah, but they are *men*—such very tedious, boring *English* men too. One of them has a sister who resembles strongly a horse, with large, yellow square teeth. She invited me to take tea with her this afternoon. I regretfully declined," he said with a graceful inclination of the head in the Gallic manner.

"You preferred Grebel's music instead?"

"When there was even a minuscule chance *you* would be there, yes. Will you share your afternoon with me?" He asked, suddenly earnest.

"I will be happy to," Laura found herself saying without hesitation. There was something about this man that intrigued her, and though she knew she was playing with fire, she could not resist.

"I have my car parked there, where it should not be parked I think, in front of someone's driveway." He seemed unconcerned, and added, "If they give me troubles, I speak French very quickly, and they just wave me away angrily. It is easy for me to find parking in London."

"You are very wily, monsieur."

"I thank you. A gentleman without wiles is like meat without sauce—dull. Do you wish to stop by to see your family? You mentioned that you saw them on Sundays."

"I had luncheon with them. Would you like to drive into the countryside or have a walk around London?"

"On such a romantic spring day we must see flowers, trees, leaves, birds. Shall we go to one of the parks and walk hand in hand like young lovers?"

"Why not, it's the season for lovers. Have you ever been to Kew Gardens?" she asked, throwing caution to the winds.

"I do not know Kew Gardens. It has trees and flowers?"

"Of all kinds. It has trees that I've never seen anywhere else. There are also twenty-four plant houses, but we won't want to go inside today, when it is so beautiful outdoors."

"You must give me directions to this place."

"The Chiswick High Road," she said, then stopped as he unlocked the door of a low-slung silver sports car.

"I didn't know it was possible to hire a car like that!" she exclaimed. "How lovely."

"Hire?"

"You said you hired a car for your visit—last night you told me."

"My associate got it for me. Perhaps it belongs to a friend. It is nice, no? My own in Paris is better. I must concede the Italians manufacture an admirable car. Mine is a Ferrari, but this is also comfortable." He unlocked her door and held it while she slid onto the leather seat.

"Do you like Ferraris?" he asked, appearing disappointed she hadn't made some comment on his owning one.

"I'm not even sure what one looks like. I don't know a lot about cars," she said vaguely.

"It is very expensive," he said.

"What a shocking show-off you are!" she teased, laughing. *"My* idea of class would be a Rolls-Royce."

"Show-off?" he asked, frowning.

"It means a boaster, and it is very common. Parvenuish," she said, attempting to translate it.

"But my family is hundreds of years old!"

"And *still* not accustomed to its wealth. One would think you'd take it for granted by now."

"English ladies are very outspoken," he commented, and they drove off.

When they arrived at the gate of Kew Gardens, he exclaimed, "This is not a garden, it is a whole city!"

"Everything from an observatory to a golf course," she agreed, "but it is the gardens in particular that are famous."

They strolled from section to section, enjoying the variety, moving from a Chinese pagoda to the Palm House, and looking at botanical specimens from all over the world.

"You can tour some of the buildings, if you'd like," she offered.

"Versailles is grander, and the Trianon is prettier," he decreed, observing the old Kew Palace. "We shall remain outside."

"We should have picked up a map. This goes on for hundreds of acres."

"I have the excellent sense of direction. We shall go this way," he told her, and struck down a path.

There were many visitors on this fine spring day, but with so many sights to be seen the walks were not at all crowded. They set a leisurely pace, talking and reading the signs that gave background of the various sights. When Henri tucked Laura's hand under his arm it seemed so comfortable and right that she didn't object.

"Look, this is nearly two hundred years old," Laura said, pointing at a false acacia with her free hand.

"I saw a glimpse of some old ruins over that way," Henri said.

She knew there were classic temples and ruins at Kew, but she hadn't thought they were visible from their walk. Henri seemed certain, however, and they rambled till they came across them—the Temple of Bellona and the Ruined Arch.

"There is something very romantic in a ruin," Laura said, gazing at the arch. "People used to build 'follies' in the olden days. These weren't true classical ruins, but were built in the eighteenth century, when people could afford such extravagant pastimes. Can you imagine anyone building a ruin today?"

"Only a fool, which is no doubt why they are called *follies,*" Henri replied.

"They remind me of Italy."

"Yes, much of Italy is a shambles, a very beautiful, romantic shambles. Greece is even better."

"I was afraid you were going to say worse."

"Ah, no, I am too French for that. I too adore follies and ruins. When you come to France, I shall show you the remains of our Roman occupation. The aqueducts are extraordinary. You can almost hear the tramp of Roman soldiers when you look at them. Such a marvel of engineering and so ancient."

"I am not going to France in the foreseeable future," she reminded him.

"In such a spot, it is easy to daydream. I could make you love France."

"It wouldn't take much work. I'm sure I'd love it."

"Why will you not come then?" he asked reasonably.

"It isn't possible at this time."

"Bah—give up the organ lessons, the Chez Nous. Life is too brief to waste it doing what we do not want."

"There are other reasons," she said mildly, thinking of the Academy.

"A man?" Henri questioned with a lift to his brow.

"No, not a man."

"You have no boyfriend, who wants to take you away from that sort of life?"

"You make me sound like a—a . . ."

"Prostitute, I think is your English word?" he questioned impassively. "I'm sorry—I see I have set you frowning. That was not my intention, but it is a hard life all the same for a young girl like you. You are exposed to many objectionable men, I think?" he asked with a sympathetic, inquiring gaze.

"Yes, but occasionally you meet a nice one too."

"Have you met this nice one?" His eyes were intent on her face as he awaited her answer.

"I think *you* are nice," she told him.

"*Merci,* mam'selle, but I did not refer to myself." Henri almost looked embarrassed for a moment, but Laura thought she must have imagined it, as his expression was once again aloof and unreadable. "You did not answer my question. Is there one particular gentleman who wishes to marry you?" he persisted.

"As a matter of fact, there is."

"You mean to have him?" he asked, observing her closely.

"No, I don't. He's only a boy really, but a nice boy. He'll make someone a good husband in a few years," she said, smiling fondly at the thought of the somewhat gawky Sean.

"In a few years perhaps he will not be offering marriage."

"You're a cynic, Henri. Growing up doesn't necessarily mean becoming a villain. I have a feeling Sean is definitely the marrying sort," she said with a pensive nod of her head.

"Sean?" he asked, getting his lips around the name with a little difficulty.

"That's his name. He's a very nice boy."

"Very much in love with 'Lovely Laura'?" he asked with a smile that hovered between mockery and teasing.

"He thinks so," she said, shrugging her shoulders offhandedly.

The mocking smile didn't fade, it vanished in one split second, replaced by an angry scowl. Suddenly his hands reached for her in the privacy of the leafy glade. His eyes were fierce. "No, Sean will not marry you!" he said with utter conviction. His tone was out of proportion to the actual situation. As though realizing it, his expression lightened. "You would not be happy with a boy," he went on in a caressing tone. "You are a woman; you require a *man*." His intent gaze left no doubt to what man he referred—himself.

His fingers bit into her arms. Before she could object, he released his hold, only to pull her into his arms. She had one brief, startled look at his face as it descended. For a man who spoke, even obliquely, of love, he looked remarkably angry. He pulled her roughly against his chest and, holding her immobile, kissed her thoroughly. Laura lost all track of her surroundings as the world disappeared in a blur of sensation, his lips bruising hers hungrily, possessively. His anger lent a sharp edge to the embrace, giving it an urgency she had not expected. That must be why her heart fluttered so disturbingly within her.

Such a kiss should have been short and fierce. She thought it would be over as suddenly as it had begun, before she could even recover from the shock of it, but instead his lips lingered on hers, the anger receding. She could sense the change as his rigid body relaxed, and his hands began to move slowly over her back, holding her in a more tender and infinitely more seductive embrace. As a new fire began to flame between them, she twisted away, unnerved by the situation and out of her depth. He resisted, clinging to her lips even as she tried to push him away.

When at last he raised his head, he still held her, his fingers twined in her hair. She felt almost as though she were looking in a mirror; for a moment both their eyes held a certain dazed wonder in them. He looked surprised and strangely vulnerable.

"Does Sean kiss you like that?" he asked when he released her, a harsh note creeping into his voice.

She swallowed and looked at him. "He doesn't kiss me at all," she said in a small voice.

"Sweet Laura, let me take you away from that place. I am wealthy. Come back to Paris with me."

"I can't," she said, shaking her head at his madness. "Please don't talk about this any more, Henri."

"You are angry with me?" he asked, his eyes shadowing.

"Do you expect me to be flattered that you ask me to be your mistress? You certainly don't use the word *marriage*."

"Does your Sean offer marriage?"

"Several times a night."

"And it is marriage you would want?"

"Of course! You don't have to think I'm loose just because I happen to play the organ at a club. Why are you looking at me like that?" she asked, as he raised his brows to observe her closely. "You don't believe me!"

"I find it hard not to believe you," he admitted in a low voice, his expression softening almost unwillingly as he gazed at her upturned face.

"Why do you try *not* to believe me? I'm afraid you're really a dreadful cynic, Henri. It must be your French blood. Let's go. Some people are coming."

He took a firm grip on her arm as they walked along.

"This is very hot, hard work, admiring all these trees. It is time for us to have a drink," he decided.

"I could use a cup of tea."

"Tea? I refer to champagne."

"You are extravagant."

"I am rich. That sliding glance tells me I am boasting again."

"I expect you'll be building yourself a folly, one of these days," she said.

"I begin to wonder whether I am not already constructing a folly," he replied half to himself.

"What do you mean?" Laura asked curiously, somewhat confused by his preoccupied air.

"Some things cannot easily be explained. Do you really prefer tea?"

"I do, and when in England, you know, you must do as the English do. There's a shop right here, on the premises."

"Laura shall have tea and even an indigestible crumpet, if it pleases her. I shall take very small sips and try to pretend I am enjoying it."

"That is magnanimous of you."

"I know."

They had their tea by a window that looked out on a garden just coming into bloom. "You may have one crumpet. I don't want you to ruin your dinner," he said sternly. "Where do you suggest I take you for our feast?"

"There are so many places . . ."

"My hotel serves an edible meal. You are familiar with the Ritz?"

"I am familiar with the facade. Is that where you're staying? You *must* be rich. They charge an arm and a leg."

"I can't understand why you are not nicer to me, since you are now convinced I have money. You are a very unusual woman. You are a seductive siren at night and a schoolgirl by day, and in both guises you do not like Henri Dufresne."

"You are mistaken. I *do* like you. I just don't like your habit of asking me to run off to Paris with you for a holiday. That's all."

"You also do not like to be in my movie. This is extremely unusual, 'Lovely Laura.'"

"I wish you'd stop calling me that. I'm not 'Lovely Laura.' I'm Laura Talmadge."

"Talmadge? Last night you were Laura Jones!" he said, his eyes snapping.

"Oh, dear, I didn't mean to tell you. It's just that I—I don't tell anyone I meet at the club who I am, you see, in case they phone me or bother me at home. It's really no great mystery."

"Your Sean of course knows your true name?"

"No, not even Sean. You're the first one I've ever told."

"Why did you tell me?"

"I didn't mean to. It just slipped out. Anyway, it doesn't matter. You don't live in London. You'll be returning to Paris soon, I expect?" she asked with a hopeful lift to her voice.

"Very soon, yes."

"When?" she asked, trying to ignore the shaft of regret that went through her at his words.

"When I have convinced you to come with me." Henri replied flirtatiously. "Where do you live, Laura?" he asked, switching from playful to penetrating in a split second.

"I'm not telling any more secrets."

"I can look it up in the phone book."

"There are many Talmadges in London."

"Many Laura Talmadges?" he asked with an arch smile.

"I don't believe you'll find even one in the book. I know I'm not there. I'm not listed."

"Why is that?"

"To prevent any enterprising person who happens to discover my name from pestering me by phone."

"Then I must continue to pester you at the club. Drink up your tea. We are leaving."

"It's not late."

"No, but we are not staying in London for dinner after all. We are going to drive along the coast and stop at a place my friend told me of. It is not fancy, but the food is good. If we go out to a London restaurant, you will want to go home and change. You will not let me drive you, so you will have to leave me, and if I let you out of my sight, I know well enough you will not return. So we are going to a place called the Red Cock, and we will have some ale and the specialty of the house, which is a chicken dish. You agree?"

"It does get rid of the bother of changing. Let's go."

It was pleasant driving in the sports car with the window open and the traffic whizzing by. "What is the name of this movie you're involved in, Henri?" she asked as they sped along.

"*Waiting for Maria*," he answered after a slight pause. "That would be the translation of the French book from which it is being adapted. We might change it."

"I would, if I were you. It's not a very gripping title."

"Suggest one."

"What's the book about?"

"Love. About a young girl who is bored in her small village and goes to Paris and later to England, becoming involved in various love affairs."

"You said last night she was an English girl," she reminded him.

"That was in hope of talking you into doing the part."

"Where does the intrigue come in?" was her next question.

"Intrigue?"

"Yes, you had said it was a story of love and intrigue. I thought it was a sort of mystery, or espionage story."

"No, no, romantic intrigue was my meaning."

She was certain it had been a mystery story he had spoken of before. It was beginning to look as if he had very little idea about the movie at all, which naturally led to the suspicion there *was* no movie. His next speech convinced her he was making up the story as he went along.

"Actually there is a run-in with a murderer. Perhaps I mentioned it to you?"

Murder had not been mentioned. He was tailoring his remarks to satisfy her. "So do you have a title to suggest?" he asked.

"How about *Maria Imaginaire*—after Molière's '*Malade Imaginaire,*' you know," she said with a pointed look.

"You suggest I invent the film to arouse your interest in me?" he asked frankly.

"It did occur to me. It's an old trick, but strangely enough, one I haven't had any personal contact with before. I guess it's so hackneyed, the men have stopped using it, just as they've stopped running out of gasoline on a date."

"Now who is the cynic?" he asked. "You are correct. There is no film at this moment, but I would be happy to produce one, if it would please you."

"What do you really do then, if you're not a producer?"

"I *am* a producer, but of beef, not movies. I also have—"

"Then you can't live in Paris, unless you graze your herd on the Champs-Elysées," she pointed out.

"I was about to say, I have other interests as well. I have an apartment in Paris, but my ancestral home is in the Moselle valley—good wine country as well as cattle. I *do* own a vineyard."

She sat silent, wondering if any of this were true, or if he was just a tourist over for a weekend, trying to impress her by inventing a fortune for himself. She was unaware of the disillusioned frown that settled on her face.

She noticed a new wariness about him as he looked at her. He looked as if he wanted to explain more, or apologize perhaps, but when he spoke, he said only, "Are you angry with me?" in a rapid, harsh voice.

"Disappointed," she sighed. What did it matter after all?

"It was a foolish lie," he rushed to say, reaching across the table to touch her hand. "I thought you would like me better if I told you that. I wanted very much for you to like me," he admitted simply. "Foolish, *non?*" The dark eyes examining her glittered with an unreadable blend of emotions.

"I wasn't impressed, Henri. I'm not one of those people who wants to be famous, or even necessarily rich. You don't get rich playing the organ, you know," she pointed out.

"There are different kinds of riches, Laura," he said softly.

It was an unlikely remark to issue from this materialist's lips, but as their eyes locked for an instant, she felt he was, for once, sincere. "I know," she answered.

Some pleasure had gone out of the day. Laura looked around. The Red Cock was a quaint country inn, the food good but not daintily served. Laura preferred its homey atmosphere to the Chez Nous, but Henri was loud in disparaging it.

"I have a poor opinion of my friend's taste, to send me here," he complained.

"Don't be such a snob. No one wants to eat escargots and lobster every day. This is a nice sauce with the chicken in mushrooms and wine."

"It pretends to be a *coq au vin*, but has all the flavor left out. The bread too is shaped like our French stick, but made, I think, of concrete."

"You must have remarkably strong teeth then. You're chewing up the concrete with no difficulty," she pointed out.

"A starving man will eat anything," he replied promptly, unfazed.

As the meal progressed, Henri asked her about her family life, and she told him of her parents' death some years before, her brother's entry into the ministry, and her efforts to educate herself. Engrossed in her story, she spoke vividly, having to blink away a tear when she remembered her mother's death and the wrenching sadness of that time. She didn't mention the Royal Academy or tell him she was still a student, but the general outline of her life was given.

Henri listened with interest. "I begin to think it is 'Lovely Laura's' story we ought to make into a film," he said, smiling indulgently with no trace of sympathy. "The orphan, supporting herself, the brother, a minister of the church. The wail of violins in the background, I think? Should there not be a villain pursuing our heroine?" he suggested playfully.

She was jolted back to the present by his insinuations. "By all means. Shall we make him a French villain?"

"Let us make him the very worst sort—French,"
he agreed. "Of course we must provide Laura a
fairy-tale ending."

"Absolutely. A prince, do you think, or would a
plain, untitled millionaire suit today's audience better?"

"Which would Laura prefer?"

"All the best heroines are marrying Greek ship-
ping magnates," she said airily. She had revealed too
much of herself already. "I could retire to a Greek
island and build a set of ruins."

"Now you are being facetious," he said, offended.

"Yes, I would much prefer an Arab sheik. They're
richer," she said with a nonchalant toss of her head.
What did she care what he thought about her? A
confirmed liar himself, he obviously thought she had
rearranged her life story to cast herself in the role of
pathetic orphan.

"One would think so to judge by the cost of
gasoline," he agreed readily, accepting her new
tack. "Which reminds me, I must fill my tank on the
way back to London."

As he finished speaking, she noticed some little
look of wariness cross his face. It was fleeting but
noticeable. What had he said or she said to cause it?
The price of gas was hardly an unusual subject for
complaint. He had to fill his tank—that too was
innocent. "My tank," he had said. It was supposed
to be a hired car. Was that why he wore that brief
look of alarm? He *did* handle the car with remark-
able ease. Wouldn't he have some difficulty locating
the various levers and handles if it were a borrowed
or hired car? It had British plates, so if it was his
own . . .

"I'll take care of the bill now. Do you want to

powder your nose?" he was saying when she
returned her attention to him.

"Yes, I'll meet you at the door."

In the privacy of the ladies' room she pondered
her problem. If he lived in England, why did he say
he was French? Was this, done to make himself
attractive to her, like pretending to be a movie
producer? If so, his aim was obviously a very
short-term relationship. She'd soon learn he had no
apartment in Paris if she were the kind of fool who
would run off with him—a virtual stranger. It began
to look as if Henri Dufresne had in mind nothing
more than a weekend affair. She felt confused, and a
little frightened—and sad, she realized. Not only did
she enjoy his company, but she found him dangerously attractive.

But when she came out of the ladies' room, she
was reassured by his respectable-looking appearance. He was well-dressed, at ease, and well-spoken.
He was no clerk out on a spree.

Chapter Four

Henri stopped at the first service station that was open. While the attendant filled his tank, he got out to check the oil and tires. Even this struck her as suspicious. Would he bother checking the oil on a borrowed car? He'd taken his wallet out to have it ready to pay. She stealthily slid it over toward her and, without even taking it in her hands, opened it on the seat, but it was too dark to read any of his identification cards. She opened the glove compartment, and a light came on. The name Richard Bowden stared at her. She could hardly believe it. She checked another card and another. Her charming French companion was undoubtedly Sean's brother. He had adopted this masquerade for some purpose of his own and had sought her out at the club.

It wasn't difficult to figure out why. Sean had

probably gone home spouting some nonsense about wanting to marry her. Perhaps his marks had arrived at Hazelhurst as well, which would bring things to a head. They held her responsible and obviously thought she was trying to inveigle him into marriage. Richard had come trying to find out what kind of a woman she was, but his mind had been made up before he got there. He thought her an adventuress, the sort who would snap at a chance to be in movies, who would gladly drop all her commitments and hop off to Paris with him for a weekend. He thought her simple enough to be impressed by his claims of owning a Ferrari car and being wealthy. No wonder he had mentioned it so often.

Whatever his true occupation might be, Laura felt he had chosen the wrong career. He was a consummate actor. His French sounded convincing to her. His attempts at lovemaking too had seemed properly ardent. Hastily reviewing her own conduct, she thought she must have convinced him she wasn't the scarlet lady they'd been imagining at Hazelhurst. Furthermore, she'd told him in so many words that she had no notion of marrying Sean. How had she come to tell him so much about her private life? He had inveigled it out of her by his insistent questioning, all done under the guise of jealousy.

Her first thought was to confront him with the wallet as soon as he returned to the car. Glancing out, she saw him wiping the dipstick and reinserting it into the tank with no suspicion of her new knowledge. But then if she said anything, she'd have to confess that she'd looked in his wallet. He'd never let her forget that small transgression! He'd think she had been trying to steal his money. No, she'd let him play out his little game and have some fun at his expense. Maybe she'd lead him on a little, let him worry about her intentions regarding his little brother. She could even see a resemblance to Sean, now that she knew of their relationship. What he was doing was an insult to a woman of good character, and she saw no reason she should let him off scot-free.

"All set?" she asked with a bright smile, when he had paid and was ready to leave.

"Almost. We have only to decide where we are to go for a nightcap. A strange phrase, *non?*" His accent, which she had found so beguiling before, now grated on her ear.

"What is the French phrase for it?" she asked.

"Odd, I don't believe we have one."

"If a good drinker like yourself doesn't know it, then there must not be one," she agreed, biting back a smile.

"I don't drink all that much," he said defensively.

"Shame on you! Isn't it every Frenchman's duty to overindulge in brandy and keep a mistress? I'm sure you told me something of the sort last night."

"Privilege, I believe, was the word. Not duty. As to keeping a mistress, it was married men we spoke of."

To further fuel her anger, she began to suspect that he had lied about being a bachelor, as he had lied about everything else. Sean so seldom spoke of his family that she knew very little about this older brother, but she *did* know he had one and complained of his interference from time to time.

"You are a bachelor, of course," she said to goad him into as many lies as possible.

"Yes, till this weekend I never met a woman I

wanted to spend the rest of my life with," he said, an oddly arrested quality to his voice.

"I'll bet you say that to all the *jeunes filles*." She retorted, refusing to let his seeming sincerity affect her.

"*Absolument non!* I never before said this to anyone. And by the way, I have preferred older women in the past, not young girls."

"But you never asked any of these old women to marry you?"

"Older! Not old. I never asked anyone that before," he insisted.

"Have you been saving yourself for me?" she asked, scarcely able to control her laughter.

"For someone like you," he told her, refusing to acknowledge her mood, but playing it straight. "You are very unusual," he added with a measuring, mystified look.

"So you mentioned. Is not wanting to be a movie star so unusual? I'm a simple old-fashioned girl. I just want to get married. Perhaps I'll accept that nice young man from the club who's always begging me to have him," she said, sliding a glance to his profile and seeing his jaw clench.

"Sean I believe the name was?" he asked, keeping his voice normal.

"Yes, Sean Bowden. He's from an excellent family, he tells me. I don't know exactly what this excellence consists of. The only one he ever mentions is his older brother," she lied in a convincing tone.

"What does he say of this older brother?" he asked with quick interest.

"Not much. He's the interfering, overbearing kind."

"The testimony of younger brothers is not always to be trusted."

"Do you have a younger brother yourself? You sound rather annoyed."

"Yes, I have. When the father is old and retired from the world, as is the case in my own family in France, the older brother must take responsibility. He tries to keep the younger from making mistakes —serious mistakes, I mean. Naturally every young fellow is going to make the conventional blunder of drinking a little too much occasionally. There is bound to be some resentment of these intrusions." She knew he spoke of himself and his brother.

"Are you considering accepting this Sean?" he asked, quickly reverting to his real fear.

"I'm considering it."

"It would be a mistake for you."

"His family would reject me, you mean?"

"Quite possibly, but that was not my meaning. You are too good for this Sean. What do you want with a green boy, a woman like you?" he asked in a reasonable, worldly tone.

"Security, a home, family . . ."

She saw him biting his lip uncertainly. She was curious to hear his next remark. "Do you love Sean?" he asked.

"No," she admitted frankly, "but he loves me."

"He is not in love; he is infatuated," he said curtly.

"Why do you say that? You don't even know him?"

"Common sense. You say he is young. He has discovered what he conceives to be an older, sophisticated woman, one touched with the glamor of show business. He would not like you nearly so well if he saw you now. My own young brother is the same, always falling into scrapes with the showgirls in Paris, where he attends the Sorbonne.''

She knew his interpretation of Sean's infatuation was accurate, but disliked being bracketed with racy Parisian showgirls. "He's very eager to marry me, at any rate," she insisted, and waited to see how he shimmied around this obstacle.

His decision was made swiftly. There was a brief, uneasy pause, then he plunged in recklessly. "So am I," he said, reaching to entwine her fingers in the darkness.

"You never said it was *marriage* you had in mind!" she exclaimed, stunned at the word. His fingers clenched hers with a spasmodic, nervous pressure.

"A man does not make up his mind to marriage in five minutes. I soon could see that you were lovely and desirable. Till I got to know you better, I thought you would make an enchanting mistress," he admitted.

"And you not even a married man!" she chided, refusing to take him seriously, though part of her insisted on fantasizing how she would feel if Richard were sincere.

"Bachelors, too, are permitted mistresses," he bantered lightly, then continued in the same vein. "But it is time I marry. All my aunts tell me so. Let us consider it, shall we?" he suggested.

"By all means, let us consider it," she agreed sweetly, but inside she was aching and utterly furious.

Actually offering marriage was going too far. It was one thing to protect a younger brother from the clutches of a misalliance—and she admitted that Sean's report of her at home must have sounded quite dreadful—but to make a proposal of marriage when you had no intention of honoring it was unconscionable. Imagine if she took him seriously and gave up her job, her studies, to say nothing of turning away a perfectly eligible suitor, whom she might be serious about for all Richard knew, only to be jilted at the last minute. But he hadn't exactly asked her to marry him, she admitted. He had only suggested they consider it. Very well, she *would* consider it and accept it before the night was through and put this impossible Richard Bowden in a totally untenable position.

"Henri," she said softly, snuggling closer to him in the car.

"Yes, *mon chou?*" His hand sought the back of her neck and stroked it gently, setting off unwilling sparks of desire.

"Do you really mean it, that you would like to marry me?"

"We are to consider it, *n'est-ce pas?*"

"For how long?"

"You will want a few days to think it over."

"You mean you're not sure," she said, adopting a pout.

His arm slid from her neck to go around her shoulders, pulling her closer to him and the color rushed to her cheeks at the warmth and intimacy of their embrace. "I want *you* to have time to think it over. It is not good to rush into these things. You might regret it. Why, it is only a moment ago you had decided to accept your Sean."

"That was before *you* said you wanted to marry me. You *did* say that." She reminded him.

"I know I did. I meant it." Richard's eyes seemed riveted to the road, unwilling to meet hers.

"That's all right then," she said with a luxurious sigh. *"I* have already decided to accept, and if you *meant* it, we can consider it settled."

"You are hasty, precipitous. 'Marry in haste, repent at leisure.' It is an English idiom, is it not?"

"I must learn French for when we go to France together," was her unsatisfactory reply to this advice.

She saw him swallow, noticed his right hand clamp the steering wheel tightly. He said nothing but only reached over to place a brief kiss on the top of her head. "I must find a spot to pull over. This is not the proper way to celebrate an engagement," he said. "Shall we go to your place?"

She was determined now that Richard Bowden must not learn where she lived. Why should she expose herself to more of his insults? "I only have a room at a boardinghouse," she told him. "I'm not allowed to have men in my room."

"That must be very inconvenient for you. Come back with me to my hotel then," he suggested. But she knew he didn't have a hotel room; he had an apartment in London. He planned to *rent* a room, and to Laura, this was tantamount to announcing his intention of seducing her. Why else did men rent hotel rooms? "We'll have a drink," he added blandly.

"It wouldn't be proper for me to go to your room alone," she said primly.

"There would be no point in your coming chaperoned. We must discover whether we are . . . compatible," he said, his tone suggestive.

"Henri!" she cried. She hardly needed to simulate the shock in her voice. So that was how he planned to get out of this hastily arranged engagement. He

would insist on his marital rights before the wedding.
That he had no intention of marrying her worsened
the case considerably.

"Have I used the wrong word again?" he asked
contritely. "We must talk, get to know all about each
other. We have many things to discuss," he said.

"A hotel room is not the place to discuss them."

"You are correct. The convenience of a bed might
prove too much temptation for us. I shall take you to
your boardinghouse, and you will meet me tomorrow in the dining room at my hotel. The Ritz,
remember? We shall spend the whole day together."

It was now time for her to direct him to her
boardinghouse. She sought wildly for some other
address than her own and finally directed him to
Francis's place.

Darkness had long since fallen. When he saw the
church next door, he pulled in to park in the lot
reserved for churchgoers. "You live convenient to a
church," he remarked.

"Yes, I have a room with the family next door."

"Is this your brother's church?" he asked.

"No, it isn't."

He turned off the lights and reached to take her in
his arms. As they were now "engaged," she could
hardly object.

"Laura, there's something I should tell you," he
said reluctantly and with a serious expression.

Her heart lifted in gratitude, thinking he was
going to reveal the whole charade. It was a chance to
clean the slate and tell him she knew all about it.
They'd share a laugh and perhaps even be friends
after. In a rush of joy she thought he was a very
considerate brother to go to so much trouble on
Sean's account.

"Yes?" It was on the tip of her tongue to add "Richard," but she desisted. She wanted him to confess voluntarily.

"I—I don't really own a vineyard," he said. His tone lacked conviction. That was not what he had been about to say. He'd changed his mind at the last moment.

"You think it's only your money I want?" she asked, her tone offended but generously forgiving.

"No! I don't know. Is it?" he asked, and gazed hard at her, his face troubled.

"That question is an insult. Do you want to reconsider some more?"

"No, I want to kiss you now," he said, his voice hoarse with suppressed emotion, as he pulled her against him in a crushing embrace. It was hard to convince herself he was acting. He ran one hand through her hair.

"Like spun platinum. Can it possibly be natural?" he asked, his voice husky.

"Everything about me is real," she answered, smiling seductively as she looked at him through her lashes. Maybe he didn't love her, but she knew he was attracted to her. She wanted him to feel some regret at least when she did not appear for their morning meeting.

"Do you really love me?" he asked, looking closely at her in the dim light of the car.

"As much as you love me, Henri. Possibly more," she admitted.

"C'est impossible!" he contradicted vehemently, and kissed her again, his lips hard and demanding on hers. French or not, he had the full Gallic share of ardor and enough of the language to be a persuasive lover. He murmured endearments in her ears, those

tender phrases often heard in popular songs. *"Je t'adore, ma chérie"* and others not so well recognized, flattering comments on her beauty, her smooth skin *comme velours,* her hair like silver silk, her lips a rosebud. All were poured over her till, even knowing what she did she felt swept by desire.

As he spoke in a soft, persuasive voice, his long fingers slid through her hair and traced the lines of her face and he placed small kisses on her eyes, her nose, the edges of her mouth. She said nothing, watching him through half-closed eyes, ruefully acknowledging that he looked strikingly handsome, his dark lashes long against his cheekbones, his strong nose and sensuous lips clear even in the filtered light. She wished she could see his eyes. She could tell a lot about a person by his eyes, and she knew she was out of her element here. She felt it a cruel prank of fate that it should have been Sean, and not this older brother, who had first come to the Chez Nous and fallen so madly in love with her. Even knowing he was insincere, she found it difficult to withstand his barrage of kisses and compliments. She turned her head aside to escape his demanding lips.

He cupped her chin in his fingers and turned her head back. "I don't think you love your Henri, *chérie,*" he said in a wistfully chiding way.

"Why do you say that?" she asked, bidding for time to gather her defenses against him.

He gazed into her uplifted face, his eyes lambent with desire, a soft smile curving his lips. "You don't return my kisses. You only let me kiss you," he told her. "I hope you are not one of the cold English women one hears of."

"To tell the truth, I'm a little frightened. I don't

often . . . do this," she said, uncertain of what phrase to use.

In the dim light she watched as his lips curved higher in a soft smile of satisfaction. "You are the sweetest girl who ever drew breath. Like a violet blooming unseen in some private glade. I am happy you don't usually do this, but you must remember you are going to be my wife. Does that not relax you?" he urged, stroking her cheek with one curved finger.

She nodded her head silently, swayed by his words, even while she knew they were insincere. His next speech, in a full-blown accent, convinced her of it.

"Kiss me then, and show me by your kiss, as you are reluctant to use words, that you *do* love me," he urged.

There seemed no way out of it, but she was determined to make it a very nominal kiss. She put her hands around his neck hesitantly and raised her lips to his, to brush them lightly like a moth wary of its approach to the flame. When she tried to withdraw, his arms jerked her tightly, convulsively, pressing her against him, till she felt one with him, fused to his body.

Her head fell back and she looked at him in rising alarm, fearful that things were getting out of her control. He was no longer smiling. He stared at her hard for a moment, as though memorizing her face or seeing her for the first time. Then he closed his eyes and kissed her. She drew a sharp breath of surprise when he parted her lips with his tongue. She tried to pull her head aside, but he made a soft, crooning sound of reassurance in his throat and held her fast, his splayed fingers cupping the back of her head. There was no escape, and soon all thoughts of escape vanished. His probing, stroking tongue excited a tingling sensation that spread like wildfire through her body, leaving her weak and breathless. When at last he ceased, she heard his rapid, shallow breaths in her ear. For a moment he held her closely to him, burrowing his face in her hair.

This time when she pulled away, he didn't stop her. She was surprised to see an expression of uncertainty on his harsh features. "That wasn't so bad, was it?" he asked softly. In her own confused state, she didn't notice for half a minute that he'd forgotten his accent.

"It was . . . perfect," she breathed, then added sadly, "I wish . . ." What she wished was that he really loved her, for she knew, to her consternation, that she had never felt like this about anyone else. It was love or passion or both, and all it guaranteed was that it would bring her pain.

"What?" he asked with seeming concern.

She shook her head. "Nothing. I wish this never had to stop. That's all." Or better, that it had never begun, she thought with uncharacteristic bitterness.

"It doesn't have to, Laura," he said huskily, his accent back in place. "But for tonight, it must be interrupted. Like our French leave-taking. We do not say good-bye; we say *au revoir*. Till we meet again, in other words. Till we kiss again. That is how I shall think of it. I love you," he said softly, sounding very sincere.

He kissed her cheek, then got out and took her to her brother's door. She was relieved to see a light on inside. She realized that if Francis had gone to bed, she would have had to end up pounding on the door in front of a very curious Richard Bowden.

"Why don't I pick you up here tomorrow?" he suggested, throwing her into alarm.

"No, no. I'll meet you at the hotel as planned."

"Ten o'clock? We'll make a day of it."

She watched as he returned to his car and left, then took a deep breath before entering the house. She told Francis and Mavis the truth—only changing the identity of her day's companion from Richard to one of the girls she had met at the concert.

"It's odd your friend didn't drive you home, since she had a car," Mavis said.

"She offered to, but when I saw your light on, I stopped here to save her the trip. She lives in the other direction and doesn't like driving at night."

"How was the concert?" Francis asked.

"Lovely. It was a lovely day," she said.

It had been too. She couldn't remember when she had had such an enjoyable day, but she was left with a bitter aftertaste knowing that Richard hadn't meant any of the nice things he'd said to her. He was only trying to reveal her as a hussy so he could tell Sean. He hadn't succeeded, so what would he tell his brother instead? She gave a mental shrug. Let him solve it and tell Sean whatever lie suited him. She was sure he wouldn't tell him the truth—that Laura Talmadge, unfortunately, had fallen in love with him.

Chapter Five

Monday was an early morning for Laura at the Academy. She went to classes as usual, though her mind strayed often to the Ritz Hotel, envisioning Richard sitting at a table waiting for her. She wondered what he would do when it finally dawned on him that she had no intention of meeting him. Would he go to Francis's house to see her? She doubted very much he could find it. It had been dark when she directed him there. He hadn't asked for an address. Even the church, which might have acted as a landmark, had been shrouded in shadows which had concealed its Romanesque style. No, he wouldn't find it—and wouldn't look very hard either, she suspected. He'd be relieved she hadn't come.

She'd made it too easy for him. He could tell Sean he had met "Lovely Laura," and found her an opportunist, ready to take up with the first man who came along dangling the prospect of a wedding before her eyes. At least he couldn't *truthfully* say she had been open to a less formal arrangement, which didn't mean he wouldn't say it anyway.

The day dragged along. Theory classes were followed by an appreciation session, in which the class listened critically to recorded interpretations of Widor's Fifth Symphony to see how the artist created his own mood by his rendition. She had lunch at the students' cafeteria and returned to the hall for her private tutorial, a part of the senior year requirement. She remained afterward, as the organ was free for student practice. She was tired but reluctant to return home.

When it could be put off no longer, she caught a bus and rode to her apartment, half expecting, even hoping, he would be waiting for her. There was no car parked nearby, no tall man loitering near the door. She made herself an omelet, salad, and coffee, and read the paper while eating it, to lessen the loneliness.

It was stupid, sitting around the apartment, mooning about a man who had treated her so very badly. She phoned Mavis to see if she would like to go to a movie as they did occasionally.

"I can't tonight, Laura. Francis is out at a meeting. It's not far from your place. He mentioned dropping in on you. How about tomorrow night?"

"I'm free. Let's meet at the Tivoli at seven. It's about halfway between your place and mine."

"What's playing, do you know?"

"An American film with Burt Reynolds."

"That's good enough for me!"

They chatted for a few minutes. There was no

mention of a Frenchman having inquired for Laura at the Talmadge residence, which set Laura's mind at rest. Still she felt slightly annoyed that he hadn't bothered to find her.

She tidied her apartment, showered, but didn't bother to put on anything but her robe, since it was growing late. She decided to have a glass of the wine Jerry had given her while she did some appreciation homework. It was on Bach's *Fantasia in C*, a favorite of hers. She listened and sipped, trying to figure out the voicing the performer had used. It was a great organ he played. Violin Diapason eight, changing to open diapason. She glanced at her hands, and noticed her nail polish needed redoing.

Hands were important in her work, and she was proud of her long fingers. She could not permit her nails to grow very long, but when she began working at the Chez Nous, she had begun using nail polish. She preferred subdued rosy tones with a pearl finish that gleamed in the light as her fingers moved over the keyboards. She heard a sound on the staircase leading to her flat and called, "Is that you, Francis? Come on in."

The door opened quietly, and Richard Bowden entered, his face wearing an angry scowl.

"Richard!" she exclaimed, and knocked over the wine glass in a convulsive movement to pull her housecoat more closely about her.

"Not the customer you were expecting, obviously," he replied with a sneer.

"Customer?" she asked, but her more immediate concern was for her attire, her intimate lack of a gown or even underwear.

She felt vulnerable with his eyes surveying her closely, sliding in a suggestive way over her long loose hair, her satin housecoat, the nail polish, and the wine bottle. Then he looked around the room at the gaudy red curtains and cheap furnishings that appeared in even worse taste in contrast to her own few good pieces scattered among them.

"I see you've devised a suitable bordello in which to entertain," he added.

His meaning became perfectly clear. He was calling her a prostitute! As she considered the circumstances in which he had found her, it was not hard to see why he thought so. Her nonchalant invitation of a man into this scene of easy domesticity must also have seemed to him additional proof, but this did not lessen her anger.

She rose in a stately move from her chair and pointed to the door. "Even bordellos have some limit. Would you please leave," she said haughtily.

"Francis would appear to be late for his appointment," he answered. "You wouldn't want to lose out on your fee. I'll take his time slot. What do you charge?"

"There isn't enough money in the world for *you* to buy my favors, Mr. Bowden."

"The prostitutes are well organized. How did you find out? Do they keep files or have a computer bank set up? Maybe you took my fingerprints."

"Nothing so esoteric. I read your name on a credit card."

"While you were rifling my wallet, no doubt. It was kind of you to leave my money intact. I didn't notice any missing, after you carried out your credit check."

His voice was quiet, but not peacefully quiet. It held a menacing note of violence held in precarious control.

"I'm not a thief and not a prostitute either, whatever you may think. How did you find my address?"

"With the greatest of ease. You aren't clever, only cunning. I drove around the block last night to be sure I could spot your place again, and lo and behold, what did I see but Miss Talmadge scampering into the night. I followed you."

"And *that* makes me a prostitute?"

"It's the right address for it. The setting, too, and the ease of entry tends to confirm it."

"Well, I'm not one!"

"Methinks the lady doth protest too much. Is it only the tardy Francis who enjoys your distinguished favors? If you limit yourself to one patron, you ought to have chosen a wealthier one. I don't think much of the love nest Francis has provided you."

"I pay my own rent, not that it's any of your business."

"Aren't you forgetting something, Laura? A fiancé generally takes some interest in who pays his bride-to-be's rent."

"The game is over, Mr. Bowden. I had no more intention of marrying you than you had of marrying me."

"But I had every intention of marrying you, my dear. *Had,* past tense. There are limits after all to what a man can condone in his bride."

"What name had you planned to put on the wedding certificate? Surely it is odd for a fiancé to be using an alias. Why, it's almost enough to make we wonder whether there isn't already a Mrs. Richard Bowden. Wouldn't *she* be interested to know where her husband spends his evenings?"

"Sorry to disappoint you. Your attempt at blackmail is futile. There is no Mrs. Richard Bowden. But we're wasting time. Francis has definitely missed his appointment," he said, walking toward her.

She backed away, looking around for a weapon to defend herself. His eyes, glittering dangerously, followed hers, while a smile of anticipation lit his face. "I can hardly wait to see how the boudoir is done up. Is it red satin, or have you opted for your other mode, the little girl look? I see some ill-advised attempts at respectability amid the garish bad taste. Gifts from gentlemen friends, I expect."

"If you so much as *touch* me, I'll call the police," she warned, her voice breathless with fear. She had reached the corner. There was nowhere else to run, with his body between her and the door.

"You've changed. Last night you wished it could go on forever," he reminded her. He took the last slow step that brought him up to her, reached out his hands, and clamped them on her upper arms. "Not to worry. You'll find me an entirely satisfying and generous *client*," he said, pulling her out from the corner.

"Don't! Please," she whispered, her eyes wide, the pupils enlarged with fright.

"Ah, now, that's more like my trembling virgin bride," he approved, but still in an angry, mocking tone. "Do you suppose you could ooze out a few tears to make it really convincing?"

"Richard, don't . . . ," she gasped, as he pulled her by main force from the room down the few steps of the hall toward the bedroom.

It was in darkness. He switched the light on with one hand, while still holding her tightly with the other. Then he closed the door and leaned against it. "Take that off," he said, nodding toward her robe.

His voice was perfectly bland but his eyes held a mixture of utter determination and deeply hidden pain.

She bit her lip to try to calm the tide of panic that was rising inside her. She felt nauseated, weak with it. How had she gotten into this awful predicament? "My brother is coming. He'll be here any minute," she said in a quavering voice. *Oh, why didn't he come?*

"Take it off," he repeated.

When she did not, he reached out and pulled the tie open. She grabbed the ends in an effort to redo them. He pulled her into his arms and kissed her with a violent, brutal passion that felt more like hate than love, or even desire. She wrestled, pushed, squirmed to get free, her breaths coming in short gasps.

"You're not getting away, Laura. You've made a fool of me for the last time," he warned, his breaths uneven. He clenched her two wrists in one hand, while shucking off his jacket from the other arm. As he switched hands to remove the other sleeve, she managed to pull free and twisted toward the door. His arm shot out and clamped her waist, pushing her housecoat aside. She felt the bite of his fingers against her exposed flesh. It affected him violently, as it did her. She quivered, trembling with fright, but with another emotion rising too.

His other arm went inside the loose coat and crushed her against him. His lips were hot, demanding. There was no delay this time before he forced her lips open and plundered the moist cavity of her mouth with his tongue. His fingers played over her back, pulling her more closely against him. A cuff link grazed her skin and she wrenched around in an effort to get free, emitting a little whimper. He only jerked her more tightly against him. It was impossible to escape. She was overwhelmed by his strength, his angry passion. The heat from his body invaded hers, stirring a quiver of unwanted response. She fought the rising fever, but her resistance was soon overcome, and she was consumed with a burning that licked through her like molten metal, hotter than fire.

Her hands, crushed against his chest, fluttered in indecision, then went around him, feeling the broad width of his back, that taut pull of muscles as he began to move against her. She pressed against him, driven by the primitive need he had ignited in her. A wild and heady excitement possessed her, driving out fear with its reckless demands.

Still kissing her, he undid his shirt, and moved her arms inside it. She touched him tentatively, then with increasing boldness, enjoying the sensuous body contact, no longer fighting him. His head flew up, and she found herself being examined by his dark eyes that stared a moment into her startled face. His cheeks were flushed, his voice hoarse, when he spoke.

"I never wanted a woman so much in my life. Witch!" he rasped, as her hands stroked his back, trying to calm him.

While she watched, hypnotized by his anger, his expression changed—slowly, like an image shown in slow motion on a screen. The anger did not fade, but it shifted and blended with other emotions: disgust, self-derision, and pain, finally resulting in a sort of angry agony.

"Richard!" she breathed, her voice catching on a sob.

His expression finally congealed to an easily recognizable fury. "No more of that!" he snarled.

She dropped her arms and stepped back, frightened.

He pulled her back against him. "Kiss me," he commanded roughly. When she didn't move, he possessed her lips himself.

His back felt like velvet and steel. She could feel the sinewy ripples of muscle, tapering to a trim waist. She felt his hands on her back sliding lower, following the sensitive curve of her waist out over the swell of hips.

She opened her eyes for an instant and saw the bed looming in the corner. It was draped not in red satin but a patchwork quilt made by her own grandmother. The original satin spread—gold, not red—had been removed. She had a fleeting thought of her grandmother and her mother and Francis.

She pushed him away. "My brother is coming," she said.

"To hell with . . ."

His words were interrupted by a tapping on the door.

"It's him!" she exclaimed.

He hastily released her, began fumbling with his shirt buttons, straightening his tie, all the while regarding her with anger leaping in his eyes. She fastened her belt, shook out her hair, and went out the bedroom door with Richard a step behind her.

"Odd a *brother* should wait to be admitted," he said, raising a skeptical brow at her. He wore his snide, sneering face again.

"It's my brother all the same," she insisted, pulling the door wide to see Chester, the cook from the Chez Nous, smiling at her.

"Hello, love," he said jauntily. "Am I interrupting something?" He looked at Bowden with lively curiosity.

"Chester, what brings you here?" she asked.

"Jerry sent me around. He's been phoning all day, but there was no answer. I can come back later if . . ."

"I was just leaving," Richard told him, with a knowing flicker of a glance at Laura. "I wouldn't want to interfere with Miss Talmadge's regular business."

"Chester is from the club," she explained.

"I expect the club is an excellent source of contacts for you. One contact will be missing in future. Sean will not be back. That's really all I have to tell you. I believe I left my jacket behind."

He turned and went into the hallway to retrieve his jacket from the bedroom floor where he had dropped it.

"Don't leave till he does," Laura said quietly.

"Is he bothering you?"

"Very much. What does Jerry want?"

"He wants to know if you're interested in playing an extra do tomorrow night. A convention from Manchester has hired the banquet room and wants some entertainment. It will be an extra fifteen quid for you, love."

"I'm afraid not. I've made plans for tomorrow night," she said, remembering her date with Mavis. It was not unbreakable, but Jerry had been asking her to play so many banquets lately that she was growing tired of it. She glanced up to see Richard had come back and was looking at her with deep disgust.

"He might go as high as twenty quid," Chester

bargained. "Shall I ask him? Nobody entertains them so well as you, Laura."

"Twenty quid! That would be for a complete performance and possibly an encore," Richard said with a blighting glare as he walked out the door.

"We are discussing *music!*" Laura called after him.

He did not turn around to acknowledge her speech, though he had to arrest his flight halfway down when he encountered one of the neighboring girls on her way up with a man at her heels.

"Who's the bloke?" Chester asked when he was gone.

"Just a . . . friend," she answered, her mind reverting to Richard's parting words.

"Well, what about tomorrow night?"

"Not this time. Sorry."

"Suit yourself. See you Wednesday." With a jaunty lift of an imaginary cap, Chester was off, whistling merrily as he descended the stairway.

She waited at the door a moment to make sure Richard did not return after he saw Chester leave. She was ready to slam it and throw the bolt if he came back, but he didn't. She locked it anyway and stood thinking a moment before going to her bedroom to get tidied up before Francis came. Tossed carelessly on the bed was a ten pound note. At first she thought it had accidently fallen from Richard's pocket, but remembered they hadn't gone near the bed. So he had *put* it there purposely; she still did not understand.

It was a few minutes before the full meaning of his gesture was clear to her. He was paying her for services rendered, as though she were a common prostitute. That was what he believed. Chester's untimely arrival, the haggling over prices, had certainly been misunderstood, confirming the idea in his mind. He would never believe the truth now— and what did it matter in any case? He had been no more serious about that proposal than she had.

She was uneasy alone in the flat. When she heard footsteps on the stairs, she waited till Francis identified himself before letting him in.

"Hi, Laura. Glad to find you at home," he said.

"I was talking to Mavis earlier. She said you might drop by."

"Can you spare a poor cleric a cup of coffee?" he asked.

"Sure, even wine, if you like."

She was sorry it hadn't been Francis who had come during Richard's visit. Her brother wasn't wearing his white collar, but even in a dark suit, he was patently respectable and patently her brother, too, with the same wide-set eyes, though his hair was darker.

"Have you taken to the bottle, Laurie? I could smell it as soon as I walked in."

"I spilt some," she said with a worried memory of what had caused the accident.

She poured Francis a glass and sat down to talk to him. She was becoming concerned about what Richard Bowden might take into his head to do next.

"You're old and wise and venerable, Francis," she said, smiling. "Give me some advice. I've fallen into a bit of a hobble at work."

She outlined the situation briefly, feeling a perfect fool, even though she suppressed the more outrageous aspects of the case.

"I worry about you at that club," he said, shaking his head in concern. "It would be best if you quit the job. Can you manage the finances without it?"

"I could scrape by, I guess. I like the work, and nothing like this has ever happened before."

"I could put more weddings and things in your way, if it would help. Which reminds me—you haven't forgotten Cousin Anne Ogilvie's wedding a week Saturday? You were going to play for it, but not for money, of course."

"I didn't forget. Maybe I should take a leave of absence from the club for a while. In a week or so the Bowdens will forget they had ever heard of me."

"Would Jerry be agreeable?"

"He'll squawk like the devil, but I'll pacify him by playing a few banquets and private parties. There's no chance of a Bowden showing up at them. Not their cup of tea—unions and such things."

"What *is* Bowden's line of work?"

"I've no idea, but I gather it's profitable."

"That still leaves you alone here, and he knows where you live now. Why not come and spend a few nights with Mavis and me? We'll move the baby's crib into our room, and let you have your old room back."

"Are you sure Mavis won't mind?"

"Lord love us, she'll be overjoyed to have some company. She misses you since you moved out. She's not a city girl at heart. She's after me to try for a country living, so she can set up as the rector's wife and know everyone in the village. I wouldn't mind it myself, to tell the truth."

"Keep a cow and a yardful of chickens?" Laura asked, smiling fondly.

"We'd have a garden at least. We'd save on greens for a few months of the year."

"Give Mavis a ring and see if I can come tonight. Bowden might be lurking around outside, waiting for you to leave," she mentioned a little nervously.

"I'll call her now, and if I see him outside, I'll pin his ears back, even if I am a man of the cloth. I believe I'll find out where he lives, and go have a chat with him. It's clear he doesn't realize you're a decent Christian woman."

"I'd rather just forget I ever heard of him."

He called Mavis, who was agreeable to the visit, and Laura packed the necessary items into a small suitcase.

The next day at noon she phoned Jerry from the Academy and said she wouldn't be in for two weeks. Jerry was loud in his scolding, till she offered to play for a few private parties and gave him her brother's number, so he could leave a message.

"I'm surprised to hear a Bowden acted so scaly," he added at the end, though he didn't really know how badly he'd acted, only that he was badgering Laura with his attentions.

"Why, do you know something about the Bowdens?" she asked with a leap of curiosity that warned her she was not so disinterested as she thought she was.

"Vera took the notion she had heard the name before, when you mentioned young Sean to her. She came across it in the papers over the weekend. It seems Bowden has bought out some company or other. He owns a dozen of them, from what the paper said."

"What kind of company?" she asked.

"It had to do with steel. He builds commercial buildings and large apartments and has bought some company that makes the girders for them. You must have heard of the Bowden Construction Company. You see their great black and white and red sign in front of half the new skyscrapers that go up in the city."

"Good grief! Is he one of *those* Bowdens?" she asked, incredulous.

"Not *one* of them; he *is* the Bowden Company. Vera showed me the picture of him in the paper, and it was the same lad who was posing as a Frenchie in here Saturday night. You should've let him pay for his own supper. He can well afford it."

"What paper was it in?"

"The *Times,* on the financial pages."

She rang off and went straight to the school library to look for Saturday's edition of the *Times.* She found the article there, accompanied by a photo of Richard in his graduation robes. There was a brief personal history included. He was the son of Sir Greville Bowden and heir to the baronetcy, which dated back to James I, and also heir to Hazelhurst, the ancestral home, famous for its fine Tudor architecture. He was a graduate of Cambridge University, and an "innovative and forward-looking designer of modern buildings, primarily for commercial uses." He had purchased a steel-rolling mill in Manchester and planned to improve its efficiency by installing modern equipment.

She was stunned to consider that such a busy and important man had devoted an entire weekend to her, till she realized his true purpose was to protect his younger brother from the clutches of a vulgar, gold-digging entertainer.

She didn't go to the club that week and didn't hear again from any of the Bowden clan. She played a schoolteachers' convention on Friday night in the banquet room and was told by Vera that Bowden, the older brother, had been in on Wednesday and Thursday evenings and had spoken to Jerry to find out when Laura would be back.

"We said we weren't sure you'd be back at all, dear, so don't worry your head about him. It's a pity he only came to make mischief, for he'd make a lovely husband, wouldn't he then?"

"Yes, for some rich daughter of a duke or earl probably," Laura answered.

"That's the truth. Money marries money, and his family is so old they'd not be looking for a mere commoner," Vera agreed rather bluntly.

Francis arranged for her to play for a wedding at his church on Saturday, and she gave the gratuity to Mavis for her board. By Sunday Laura felt she was safe from further interference from the Bowdens and returned to her own flat. Francis and Mavis had asked her to stay for another week, but there is a limit to anyone's hospitality, and Laura decided to leave.

"We'll see you next Saturday for Cousin Anne's wedding," Mavis reminded her. "What are you giving for a present?"

"I haven't decided. What are you and Francis giving?"

"A silver-plated teapot. There's a milk pitcher and sugar pot to go with it. We could go in together, the three of us, and give her the set."

Laura dug into her purse to pay her share and then was off home. She carefully locked the door behind her this time and unpacked her valise, sorting the clothing into piles for washing and hanging up. The laundromat was open on Sundays and usually wasn't busy that day, so she made up a bundle to take around the corner, taking a novel with her to pass the time.

She had put all thought of the Bowdens out of her mind by the time she got home. Certainly Sean had nearly ceased to exist for her, so that she didn't immediately recognize him, lounging against a bright red car by the curb. Sean had frequently complained of not owning a car.

He came bolting down the street to meet her. "Laura—let me take that bundle. You shouldn't have to carry such bulky things. What the deuce is it?"

"Sean, what are you doing here?"

"I have to talk to you."

"Are you alone?" she asked, with a suspicious look into the red car.

"Yes, I've just returned from Hazelhurst. I've been talking to Richard."

"You know what happened, then."

"It is the most outrageous thing I ever heard in my life. I want to apologize for my brother's behavior."

"How did you know I live here? Did he tell you?"

"He wouldn't tell me, but I knew *he* had been here and found your address in his black book. I meant to camp on your doorstep till you came back."

"We can't very well talk on the street. Come on up," she invited.

"We could talk in my car," he mentioned with a covetous smile at the flashy red thing.

"I have to fold my laundry."

He followed her upstairs to her rooms, looked

around with a critical air, and said, "I knew it couldn't be as bad as he said."

"What did he say?" she demanded, her voice thin with anger.

"He said it was the nest of a bird of prey, trimmed out in cheap, tawdry knickknacks and red curtains to seduce youngsters. He called me a *youngster*, imagine!" he exclaimed, this being by far the greater insult in his reckoning.

"Kind of him! Sit down and make yourself comfortable while I fold my things. Do you want some tea?"

"Tea? You served Richard wine," he pointed out.

"I did not serve Richard anything."

"He said the whole place reeked of wine."

"That was because he made me spill my glass."

"Then you *were* drinking wine!"

"I wasn't *serving* it," she said impatiently. "Do you want the tea or not?"

"No, thanks. Anyway, I have come to tell you that I still want to marry you, whatever he may say. I bought the car without his consent too. They let me borrow against my trust fund at a loan company. I'll be coming into a great deal of money from Uncle Artemis when I am twenty-five, and there's no way Richard can stop me from marrying whomever I want."

"I'm tempted to accept out of spite, but that is a poor reason for marrying anyone. I have told you several times, Sean, that I'm not interested in marriage."

"You would have married *Richard*. He said so."

"I only said it to vex him. I wouldn't marry him if he were inlaid with diamonds, and you can tell him I said so."

"Of course he never intended to have you. It was a cheap trick to show me what kind of woman you are. It doesn't bother me. I'm sure there is a very good reason why a woman adopts this sort of life. No one would be a call girl if she had any other choice."

"Let's get something straight," she said, snapping a pillow case to vent her frustration. "I am not a call girl. Since your brother and you have such an overweaning interest in my life, I will tell you, I am a student. Yes, a *student*, Sean, like you."

He blinked in disbelief. "You don't have to lie to me, Laura. I don't care what you've been in the past. After we are married, you'll . . ."

"I am a student. I study the organ at the Royal Academy of Music."

"But how can a woman your age be a student?" he asked.

"My age is twenty-one, not a hundred."

"Twenty-one? You're only a year older than *me!*" he exclaimed, examining her face closely for signs of more advanced years, and frowning when he couldn't find them. "You *do* look a lot younger without your nice eye shadow on. Do you—do you usually dress like this when you're not at work?" he asked with an air of disenchantment creeping into his voice, as he looked at her plaid, pleated skirt, tailored blouse, and flat-heeled shoes.

"I don't wear long gowns and rhinestones to do my housework," she said sharply.

"There's no reason to be snarky with me. You were always so sweet-tempered, Laura."

"Yes, and look where it got me. I had to give up my job, which I not only liked but needed. I had to move out of my flat, and I've been insulted in every imaginable way by your brother."

"He is impossible. He's bent on ruining my life as well, wanting me to go on and finish that dull university course. I want to be a movie director," he added wistfully. "He knows it perfectly well. I've often told him so. In fact, it was a dream of mine to star you in my first production."

"So that's where he got the idea!"

"What idea?" he asked.

"Never mind. It doesn't matter."

"Did he make you promises? Did he ask you to be in a movie?"

"Yes."

"That was *my* idea!" he shouted, flinging out his arms, and knocking over a lamp that rested on the table beside him. "I told him *I* was going to ask you, because everyone knows all entertainers really want to be in movies. You're right, Laura. He's treated you badly, and I want to make restitution. You'll look as lovely as ever when you put on some makeup and a decent outfit."

"You don't love me, Sean. You love mascara and stage paint. You love long, slinky gowns, and cheap romance. And I don't love you either, so let's stop being ridiculous."

"There's no reason to take it out on *me*, because Richard insulted you. I'm making my offer in good faith. I'll marry you. I said I would," he added grudgingly. "I am a Bowden. A gentleman does not go back on his word, and in a way I suppose it's my fault you lost your job."

"Don't do me any favors," she said harshly. "Except one. Go away and don't come back."

"I *will* come back, but I'll give you time to simmer down first. Your terrible temper is understandable, considering what you have been through. What I *don't* understand is why Richard is in such an almighty rage. *He* got what he wanted or *thinks* he did. He acts as though he were my father. I don't plan to knuckle under to him. I'll marry you if I want to."

"That will be quite a trick, without my consent."

Sean rose and looked sadly about the room. "I didn't picture you living in a place like this," he said. "I pictured you in a French villa with a pond at the door, willows drooping gracefully over it, and a pair of black swans floating idly by."

She picked the shabbiest article out of her laundry —a dust rag—and shook it out. He regarded her, disillusionment on his youthful features. "It could still be like that," he said, ambling toward the front door, and tripping on the doormat before he got out, ruining his nonchalant exit.

As soon as he was gone, she rose and put the lock on, shaking her head at his foolishness. Poor Sean. She shouldn't have taken her anger out on him. He was only a young, dreamy romantic. He no more loved her nor really wanted to marry her than he wanted to go to his university. She finished folding her laundry and putting it away without further interruption.

She passed the evening by cleaning her apartment, dusty from the week's absence, making a list of groceries to be replenished, then showered and went to bed.

She was dissatisfied with the termination of the Bowden affair. Richard had got it all his own way. He had successfully severed the connection between

Sean and herself, which did not bother her a hoot; it even pleased her—what annoyed her and plagued her like a toothache was that all his various insults had gone unpaid and unanswered. She shouldn't let him get away with it, but could think of no means of retaliation. It was all over, finished, and the only satisfaction she had was in knowing Richard was in a rage too—or so his brother said.

Chapter Six

On Monday Sean Bowden was waiting outside the Academy when Laura came out of her last afternoon class.

"We've got to talk, to make some plans," he said in an earnest, determined way.

"Get lost, Sean," she said, using the bluntest terms possible to get rid of him and kept walking.

He tagged along beside her, outlining his plan. "What we have to do is get a special license. You're of age, so it won't be any problem. If we get a license, Richard won't know a thing about it till it's over. He won't be able to stop us."

"Forget it," she said, still walking.

"If you like, we can wait till your term is over. It's only a few weeks. It might be best to wait."

"I'm not marrying you. Not now. Not ever. Period."

"You have to. You've lost your job. You're an orphan, and it is all my fault. Not that you're an orphan, I mean, but losing your job. And your brother a poor cleric, unable to be of the least help. God only knows where you'll end up. Walking the streets in some slum, degrading yourself, selling your favors for the price of a meal. I have to marry you," he said with a noble expression worthy of the stage.

She realized he had changed her role from scarlet woman to destitute orphan in order to lend some romance to the affair. His bent for melodrama required it.

"I have some money. My brother also has enough to toss an occasional bone into the snowbank for me, come winter. I don't need your charity."

"I'm glad to see you have your pride. I know you love me and don't want me to lower myself by this match, but really, Laura, that *proves* you love me. Don't you see? You're putting my interest before your own."

"In my own self-interest, I wouldn't have you on a platter. I don't love you, never did, and am rapidly coming to dislike you very much."

"There goes your bus," was his reply to this assertion. "Let me give you a drive home at least. You've never been in my new car."

"All right, you owe me that much, but you're not coming in."

They walked to his parked car, Sean's shoulders going back and his chest out as he smiled at the shining paint and chrome.

"What does your brother think of your wanting to go ahead with a marriage?" she asked, her tone ironic.

"He threatens to have me committed to an insane asylum if I do it."

"Nice to know I'd be welcomed with open arms at Hazelhurst."

"We wouldn't go near the place. I've met a fellow at the university who is going to Italy to help make a film this summer. He's only doing some accounting work for them, but it's a connection at least. Once we got there, and they saw how beautiful you are, they'd hire you to play a role. Of course you'd have to wear your makeup and decent clothes," he advised her with a disparaging look at the gray flannel slacks she wore.

"I don't have any decent clothes," she answered at random, then held on to the seat's edge as Sean squealed on to the road, driving as awkwardly as he walked.

"I'd groom you," he countered. "It's done all the time. A talented director takes a plain girl and turns her into a legend. Look at Roger Vadim, who created Brigitte Bardot and Jane Fonda and a whole raft of women."

"It would never work. I have bowlegs," she told him, to squash this latest absurdity before it got out of hand.

"No, you haven't. I noticed yesterday you have very nice legs. You wore that childish kilt, remember?"

"You can let me out here. I have to buy some groceries," she said when they approached her neighborhood.

"I'll help you," he said, and insisted, in the teeth of all her loud opposition.

He clearly expected to be invited in to dine with

her after carrying two large bags of groceries up
the stairs to her rooms. "Thanks a lot," she said at
the door. "You can just put them on that table
and leave."

"But—but you bought two steaks," he reminded
her.

"Yes, one for tonight, and one to be frozen for
later in the week. Good-bye, Sean. See you at the
movies."

"I'll get to work on it," he said. "I'll be in touch
with you soon."

"Thanks for the warning."

She closed the door after him and locked it, trying
to decide which of the Bowden brothers was the
more impossible. She cooked her steak, ate alone,
and discovered that she wanted some company. She
phoned a girl from her class who brought over some
records. She listened more closely for a telephone
ring than to the records, but when a call finally came,
it was only Mavis telling her she'd got the silver tea
set and asking whether she could borrow a black
purse for the wedding. The evening was curiously
flat. Why did she keep thinking Richard would
phone or come? If he did either one, it would only
be to heap more insults and abuse on her. Still she
felt definitely let down when she finally went to bed
without hearing from him.

Richard made up for his neglect the next day. She
got home from the Academy without encountering
Sean, only to find Richard sitting in the plush chair,
listening to her records, with a glass of her wine in
his hand, half-drunk, indicating he had been waiting
for a while. She realized she was not at all frightened, but felt strangely exhilarated.

He turned his head slowly to regard her from cold, dark eyes. He did not arise to acknowledge her entrance. Remembering the alacrity with which he used to hop up before, she recognized this as a calculated insult.

"Don't bother to get up," she said ironically. "Have you taken up breaking and entering to enliven your dull days?"

"My days are far from dull. The janitor was happy to let me wait for my cousin after I gave him a large tip. Letting gentlemen in to wait seems to be an accepted custom in this building. You women should get together and provide a waiting room."

"*You* would know how the matter is handled in houses of ill repute, no doubt."

"It has been my experience that money smooths the way, there as elsewhere."

"Your piles of money make life easy for you, don't they, Mr. Bowden?" she asked, setting her purse on a table and opening it to extract the ten pound note he had thrown on her bed. She tossed it toward him. "You *accidentally* left a little of it behind, last time you were here."

He allowed it to flutter to the floor at his feet without looking at it. "On the contrary, it makes life difficult. It attracts the attention of the greedy and immoral," he said, his voice cold, his eyes regarding her as though she were a worm.

"If your kind phrase refers to myself, you are mistaken. Sean did not attract my attention; I attracted his. He has pursued me for several weeks now. I never asked *you* to harass me either."

"Didn't you accept the offer of a total stranger, who was at no pains to conceal his intentions?"

"I accepted one drink to get rid of you."

"Cut line. We both know why I'm here."

"I haven't the faintest notion why you are here. Please state your business and leave."

"You have succeeded in alienating Sean from me and the rest of his family. Under your influence he has neglected his studies, gone into debt to buy a car, and now speaks of marrying you and going to Italy to be a clerk."

"But eventually a movie producer!" she pointed out. "He has ambitions. That particular trait seems to run in the family."

"We both know it's money you're after. If you have any conscience at all, you'll take the money and let Sean go. What's your price?"

Her heart thudded slowly, heavily, as she looked at this supercilious, haughty, and arrogant man, who had devised yet another insult. She felt suffocated by fury. "You are offering to buy me off?" she asked, lest she had misunderstood his meaning.

"Precisely. What sum will you take to disappear from our lives?"

"It must be nice to be rich. I wish I could afford to buy *you* off to butt out of *my* life."

"No doubt you've determined the exact extent of his fortune. You also must know he doesn't gain control of it till his twenty-fifth birthday. Five years is a long time to wait to get your hands on it. I'm offering ten thousand, cash, for you to leave town without seeing him again. You will sign a document acknowledging this payment. I won't show it to Sean unless you return. It is a sort of insurance policy to let him know exactly what you are. I think even *his* infatuation might be cured by that."

He rose and handed her a certified check for ten thousand pounds. She accepted it, smiled at the sum, and tore it into small pieces. *"That* is what I think of your paltry offer, Mr. Bowden," she said.

"It's a generous offer. You won't get a penny more."

"Why the diamond ring I refused was worth more than this."

"True, but the diamond ring was entailed. It belongs to the estate in perpetuity and could not have been turned into cash. I'm sure that occurred to an experienced adventuress like yourself."

There was no way she could win this battle, but she could cause Richard a few days of worrying at least and was strongly of a mind to do it.

"Yes, one of my broad experience in fleecing minors would be hardly unaware of such matters. I also know I can get my hot little hands on the whole fortune once he is twenty-five. I am only twenty-one myself, you know. I will still be young enough to enjoy it in five years. Meanwhile . . ."

"Meanwhile you'll have slim pickings. His estate is under *my* control, and he won't get a penny!"

"As I was about to say when I was so rudely interrupted, meanwhile Sean is going to make me an international sex symbol in the movies," she answered with a triumphant smile.

His face assumed a livid hue, which encouraged her to expand on this theme. "Laura Bowden, the new British "10." But don't worry that I might disgrace your old, prestigious family. My brother, the cleric, wouldn't permit it. I will absolutely refuse to do nude scenes—unless they should be really necessary to the film, of course. What is your view on centerfolds, Mr. Bowden? Do you think they are tacky? *I* think if we just put the family crest in strategic places in lieu of a fig leaf, it will raise the tone, don't you?"

He jumped to his feet, looking ready to strike her. In two long strides he was beside her, his face a pale mask towering above her. "If you attempt anything of the sort, I'll sue you for contributing to the delinquency of a minor."

"Tsk, tsk. I shall countersue for alienation of affection. Really, a mere ten thousand pounds. You must take me for an *amateur!*"

"What *is* your price? I begin to think I would give my last penny to be rid of you."

"Now that's more like it! You're beginning to be reasonable. What did you pay for the steel mill you bought in Manchester last week?"

"You've done your homework well."

"I couldn't be bothered wasting time on a family with a mere million or so. What do you say to fifty thousand?"

"I could have you killed for less than that and do the world a favor!" he exclaimed, but she saw he was considering this outrageous offer.

"A *double* favor, if they put you away too," she smiled sweetly.

"Fifty thousand is out of the question. We might strike a compromise. Say . . . twenty-five thousand," he suggested, flinging a hand into the air.

"It doesn't do to make important decisions hastily. You told me so yourself on another occasion. Why don't we sleep on it?"

He looked at her, a sharp, questioning look, a strange flicker in his eye. "Each in our own separate beds, I mean. I only give organ lessons, no other kind," Laura added swiftly, her voice catching at the thought of Richard's body close to hers.

"It's pretty clear which organ of the body you perform on. I wish my brother had heard this discussion."

"I wish I'd thought to tape it!"

"Do you also film your sexual encounters to blackmail your partners?"

"Hardly ever, but it's an excellent idea."

He made a growling sound and pounced toward the door. "I'll be in touch with you tomorrow."

"You forgot your ten pounds, Mr. Bowden," she called, pointing to the note on the floor.

"I didn't care to touch it, after it's been in your hands," he answered sneeringly, then left.

She was strangely reluctant to touch it herself. It and the torn check remained on the floor all evening, receiving frequent looks of opprobrium from the irate, frustrated Laura.

How *dare* he make such an offer to her? She could have had his stupid brother for the taking, and that was still true after she had done everything in her power to make Sean dislike her. She should marry Sean yet to teach him a lesson. She envisioned a life of taunting the lofty Richard Bowden by her immoral exploits, till she realized how very much she would hate such a wanton existence. Next she began to consider what she would do when and if he actually appeared at her door with a check for twenty-five thousand pounds. Twenty-five thousand pounds! How very much he must hate her, if he would really pay such a fortune to be rid of her. And to cap the situation, it was all *their* fault, his and Sean's.

All she had done was to be kind to a college boy

who had been infatuated with her and kind to a man she had mistaken for a lonely stranger in England. That was what came of being kind to people. She would have to tell him she wanted nothing from him; she never wanted to see either of them again. She'd pay twenty-five thousand not to, if she had it.

On Wednesday Sean was waiting outside the Academy. She saw him through the glass door and turned around to leave by the rear exit. She took a bus to Francis's house and remained there for the evening. On Thursday there was a curt note from Richard, written by hand on his office stationery, telling her he would meet her Friday afternoon at three at his office to finalize the transaction as agreed upon earlier. No price was mentioned. She read the letter, her chest heaving with righteous indignation. She phoned him to give him a piece of her mind and was told by his secretary that he was at a meeting. She was asked to leave her name and number, but refused.

On Friday she didn't go to the meeting he'd arranged. Her classes finished at noon and she could have gone without even cutting a class—not that *he* would have known or cared—but she didn't. She went home instead and locked the door, determined not to admit either Bowden. Her phone began ringing at three fifteen and rang every ten minutes for an hour. She knew it was Richard or his secretary and fully expected he would come banging down her door. She dressed in her most sedate black and white dress to make him feel really cheap for having misjudged her when she returned his check, but it was all in vain. He didn't come.

She played a private party for Jerry in the banquet room on Friday night and took a taxi home, half expecting to see one of the Bowden cars parked in front of her flat. There was no car, nor any man waiting for her in her living room. What could have happened? Had Richard finally been convinced of the truth—that she was no menace whatsoever to him and his brother? Or was he busy arranging some new insult? She even wondered if she might receive a visit from the law, but none came.

Saturday she had her cousin Anne's wedding to play for and the reception to attend after. Francis and Mavis invited her to stay overnight at their place, and in a fit of despondency she accepted. Time hung heavy on her hands without her club work. It was to be an afternoon wedding, and Laura dressed after a late lunch. Since the weather was warm and sunny, she chose her navy blue silk suit. It fit tightly at the waist and had a straight, slit skirt. The only problem was that she had no hat to go with it. She rolled her hair up in a French knot and attached a pink silk rose at the back to peep out over her ear in front. She packed her weekend bag, then decided to call a taxi rather than haul the bag on and off the buses. She collected the necessary rice and confetti, then reached for the phone.

Before she lifted the receiver, there was a sharp knock at her door. Her heart leapt. *Richard!* she thought at once, and regretted that she didn't have time to talk to him. In the few seconds between hearing the knock and reaching the door, she pictured him contrite, having learned the truth. He would drive her to the wedding, while she explained any details that had eluded him. She even had time to picture him calling for her after the wedding and going out with her for a drink or dinner. In her mind's eye it was to the Chez Nous they went, for old time's sake, to laugh over the tempest in a teapot.

"Sean!" she exclaimed, her hopes dashed as she saw the gangly youth lounging in her doorway, perspiration on his brow, his jacket dangling from his fingers. He came in and dropped the jacket on a chair.

"Hello, Laura. I suppose you wonder why I've been so long getting in touch with you. I've been hanging around the Academy and phoned you several times, but could never get hold of you. Have you been hiding from me? Richard thinks so. He thinks you're trying to scare me by playing a little hard to get." He smiled to see her looking like her old self with her hair up and wearing an elegant outfit. A quick peep at her ankles confirmed that she was not bowlegged at all, just as he had thought.

"Don't talk to me about your brother," she ordered, then immediately added, "I hope you set him straight."

"I did," he assured her. He picked up the bag of confetti and frowned at it. "I told him nothing would prevent me from marrying you, but our trip to Italy is off. I got an interview with the Italian film people, and they suggested I finish my course before going to work. I suppose we'll have to stick it out in London next year, but it'll be only for a year. There are plenty of films made right in London. We'll work out something."

"There won't be any made by *me*."

"I'm not trying to get out of my offer to marry you, if that's what you think. I said I would, and I will. If you want to wait till I'm through school, however, it might be a good idea. I mean, to have to

pay for an apartment for two out of my allowance.
. . . I live with Richard now, you know, and that
doesn't cost me anything. An apartment costs an
arm and a leg. I've been looking them up in the
classified ads. I went to see a few, but what I can
afford would be nearly as bad as this. My brother
says he won't let me have a penny more than my
present allowance till I'm twenty-five. In fact, I'll
have less, as he's making me pay for my car loan out
of it too."

"Relax. I don't plan to marry you. I have to go,
Sean. I'm late for a wedding already."

"Whose wedding?" he asked suspiciously. "I
noticed you were looking well today." As he spoke,
his nervous fingers played with the bag of confetti.

"My cousin. I'm playing the organ for it. I have to
be there early. I play while the bride comes down the
aisle. I really have to go. I was just about to call a
cab when you came."

"I'll drive you. I've nothing planned for this
afternoon. It's the least I can do."

"All right. I just have to get my gloves. Be careful
with that confetti and rice, will you? It's a nuisance
to clean up if you spill it."

He obediently set it down, as he had punctured
the bag with his thumb. A few bits of the confetti
already littered the floor, but he kept his feet over
them so she wouldn't see.

"I'm ready," she said a minute later. "Let's go. I'll
direct you to the church." She remembered the
confetti and noticed the hole in the bag when she
picked it up. A puddle now sat on the table. "Thanks
a lot, Sean," she said through her teeth as she
wrapped a tissue around the punctured bag.

Sean was so busy feeling clumsy that he left

without picking up his jacket from the chair. The woman from the next apartment was climbing the stairs as they left. Sean regarded the large, flamboyant redhead with approval.

"Hi, Laura. You're all dressed up today," she remarked.

"We're on our way to a wedding," Laura answered. She was always polite to her neighbors, but her suspicions of their nocturnal activities prevented any close friendship.

"Do people still get married? How quaint," the woman replied, running her eyes over Sean in a manner to please him. "You're not the groom, I hope?" she asked boldly.

"Me? No, oh, no!" he assured her.

"Good. See you around sometime." The woman went on up the stairs, while Sean turned to stare after her.

Sean drove badly. In his mind was an image of a racing driver, bent over the wheel, but the only part of this image that came through was his speed. He drove too quickly through the heavy traffic but did reach the church without accident.

"We're late. The bride is just pulling up. I'd better get up into the choir loft right away," Laura said.

Sean held the door, his eyes resting on the vision in white that emerged from the automobile. There was enough romance attached to a wedding to make him want to stay. "I think I'll just go in and watch it," he said to Laura.

"Without a jacket?" she asked.

"I've got two in the back of the car. I was taking them to the cleaners."

By the time she had unlocked the choir, he'd caught up with her, jacket in place. "Can I go upstairs with you? It won't bother you, will it? You never know when you might have to film a wedding scene. It's good to know how an average wedding is carried out."

"You can stay, but don't talk to me. I have to concentrate."

His eyes found Laura attractive enough to occupy him while he waited for the wedding procession. He stood on a raised step designed for the choir, so that he looked down on her long lashes fluttering against her cheeks. She had her hair done in an intricate and sophisticated swirl that looked like a pinwheel. The dark silk rose cast an interesting shadow against its silvery paleness. To add a thoroughly striking note, the stained glass cast multicolored splashes of light over her and the organ. This would be a marvelous effect in a movie, he thought.

Laura looked into the mirror suspended over the organ to see Francis give her the signal to begin the music. The solemn, sonorous notes of *Lohengrin* rose to reverberate through the crowded church. The heads of the collected guests turned back for a look at the bride as she paraded with slow, stately steps up the aisle on her father's arm. Sean stood transfixed in pleasurable musings.

When the ceremony was finished, Laura played again as the bride came back down the aisle, now on her groom's arm, both of them wreathed in smiles. A lump formed in her throat as it always did at this magical moment. There was something awe-inspiring to consider the faith and trust and love shared by two who agreed to spend their lives together as one. She wondered wistfully if it would ever happen to her.

"I'm going down to watch them come out of the church," Sean said in a whisper and disappeared, while she played on as the crowd began to file out after the wedding party.

As she gathered up the music, Francis came up to the loft. "They're going to take some pictures in front of the church, then go on to the church hall for the reception. I'm going over there now to see that everything is ready. It went well."

"It was lovely. I'm always afraid someone will stand up and cause a ruckus when you come to the bit about 'speak now or forever hold your peace.' Has it ever happened to you?"

"Not so far. I wonder what a minister is supposed to do if it does."

"Don't *you* know?" she asked, laughing.

"I've no idea. I fancy I'd just have to hear him out and decide whether he was a lunatic or what. Oh, by the way, I have a new piece here I'd like you to give a try tomorrow at the service. Folks get tired of the same old tunes forever."

He handed her a folder of music, and she perused it with interest, noticing it was not too difficult. "I'd like to give it one try before Sunday," she decided.

"Do it now if you like. They'll be taking pictures for a while. I have to run."

He left, and she played the new hymn through once. There was a time change midway through that she played once more to ensure a flawless performance next morning. Before she finished, Sean had come back up to the loft.

"They've gone off to the church hall. What a beautiful bride she is. Do you know her?"

"She's my cousin, Anne Ogilvie. Anne Norris

now. How strange to think of her being a wife. She was always such a tomboy."

"She looks like an angel," he sighed. "Weddings are beautiful, aren't they? The ritual, the pomp, the music, the flowers. I picked you a flower to wear to the wedding party. Many of the women have corsages. Why don't you have one?"

"Because I'm not the bride or a bridesmaid," she said, tucking the daffodil into her lapel and noticing he had helped himself to one of Francis's early blooms as well. "Where are you going now, Sean?" she asked.

"Home, I guess, after I drop my clothes off at the cleaners. What shall I do with your suitcase?"

"I'll leave it at the rectory. I'm—" She stopped, because she hadn't planned to reveal to him where she was spending the weekend.

"What?" he asked.

"I'll pick it up there after the wedding party."

"Are you going away for the weekend?"

"No," she answered. He did not bother to question why she had brought a bag, which showed pretty clearly that he had lost real interest in her and her doings.

"You're serious about not wanting to marry me?"

"Perfectly serious. Let this be the end of our . . . affair," she said, disliking the word, but not able to find another that suited any better.

"The end of the affair," he said, smiling sadly. "You're right. It wouldn't have worked out. I'm sorry for all the trouble I've caused you, Laura."

"That's all right."

They went down the steps together into the dark vestibule, where only one small window in the choir loft door gave any light at all. "You know, Laura, after all the time I have been in love with you, I never once kissed you."

"No, you never did. Would you like to kiss me good-bye?" she asked, feeling some premature sense of loss at the final exit from her life of Sean Bowden. He had been a terrible nuisance but never a bore.

"Yes, I would. Just one, to end the affair," he said, and put his arms around her shoulders lightly. He kissed her on the lips, but it was fleeting—a chaste peck, very unlike those ardent embraces she'd shared with his brother.

Then he put his hands on her shoulders and looked down into her face. "I never thought—" The sentence was not completed.

The door was pulled violently open from outside. Towering in the sudden shaft of light was Richard Bowden. His face was in total darkness, but his mood was evident in the stiff set of his shoulders, the rigid angle of his head. Sean dropped his hands and turned toward the door. "Richard!" he exclaimed guiltily.

Laura just looked at that outline and knew there was going to be a dreadful scene enacted in the sanctity of the church if she didn't do or say something to forestall it. It even seemed possible the two men might come to blows.

"You'd better go, Sean," she said quickly.

"I'll get your suitcase," he said, and edged out past his brother, who turned his head stiffly aside to glare at him.

"I'll deal with you later," Richard threatened. The door closed, returning the vestibule to its usual gloom.

"We can't talk here," Laura said, and took a step toward the door. A hand fell on her upper arm. It felt like a ton of lead.

"Not so fast," Richard growled, and swung her around to face him.

In the gloomy, airless anteroom, his features assumed the menacing aspect of a devil's mask. His eyes were two black holes, his lips a gash.

"You may think you've bested me, but I haven't begun to fight. I'll have this travesty of a wedding annulled so fast your head will spin. You won't get the twenty-five thousand, and you won't get Sean. All you'll get for your scheming is public exposure for the vulgar, fortune-hunting, cradle-snatching tramp you are. I'm a poor loser. I've spoken to my lawyers, who assure me there is such a thing as entrapment. You entrapped my brother."

"You misunderstand. I didn't—"

"You did!" he contradicted baldly. "You ensnared him."

"You're making a big mistake," she protested.

"You've made a bigger one," he shot back. He was livid with fury, with a whiteness about the lips that accentuated it. "You really slipped up this time, Laura. *I'm* the one with the money, and that's all you're after. Sean hasn't made his fortune yet, and he's not the heir to Hazelhurst either. It's entailed on the elder brother—me. Sean has no more than a competence."

"I didn't . . ." she began indignantly, but was too disheartened to continue.

He stared for a moment, then said in a reluctant, strained way, as though dragging the words out, "There's just one detail that continues to puzzle me. Why did you keep after Sean, when you had an offer of marriage from *me?* You had me in the palm of your hand, ripe for plucking, in spite of my better judgment. You knew who I was. You called me Mr. Bowden when I went to your flat the first time. You knew I was rich. So why did you choose Sean over me?" There was a world of hurt behind the anger of the question, but Laura was too angry herself to hear it.

"I didn't have an offer from Mr. Bowden. I had a trick played on me by Monsieur Dufresne. I can play tricks too."

"You've out-tricked yourself this time. I was besotted enough to marry you, even though I knew it was the money you were after. So is every other woman I go out with. You weren't different in that respect. Oh, and your act was *very convincing*. 'I'm so frightened. I don't do this,' with the lashes fluttering and the lips trembling. You do it remarkably well for someone with no experience. I'd never met a professional virgin before. The only reason I'm telling you this is so you'll feel the sting of remorse at having lost out on the richer man."

The room felt cold. She shivered and drew back a step from him, but his fingers strained against her wrists till the bones ached. "I wouldn't marry you if you had a billion pounds. If you owned the world, I wouldn't have you. You're *obscene!*" she said, her voice cracking at the weight of emotion she was holding back, her fantasies of a reconciliation in ashes at her feet.

"That's pretty good, coming from *you!* I'm taking Sean home to Hazelhurst. If you come near him, I'll have you arrested for trespassing. You'll receive the annulment notice in the mail. If you don't get a warrant for your arrest at the same time, you can count yourself lucky. I never want to see you again. I don't want to hear your name spoken. I'm leaving now, before I lose control and strangle you."

He flung her hands away and stalked from the church vestibule. She felt weak and shaken from the awful encounter. She went into the church and just sat in the back pew, trembling. It wasn't till she had reviewed the ordeal twice that her anger began to subside and regret seep in to replace it. 'You had me in the palm of your hand.' It couldn't be true that she had come that close. But she knew it was. Richard wouldn't have been in such a fury over her fooling Sean. That degree of emotion had to concern himself.

Gone. She'd never see him again. She felt empty, too drained even for tears. She felt as if she'd lost a limb, some vital part of herself, that made her unable to face the world.

Chapter Seven

Later, Laura had only the vaguest memories of that
wedding party. She'd straggled in late and spoken to
friends and relatives she hadn't seen for some time.
Francis told her she was pale and got her a glass of
wine. While happy voices buzzed around her head,
she heard over and over the harsh, damning words
of Richard Bowden. She had been too stunned to
be as angry as she should have been. She hadn't
known such violent hatred existed. It even seemed
possible he might have strangled her, if he'd remained longer.

Of course no annulment notice arrive in the mail.
How could it? Obviously Sean had told Richard the
truth, and she felt Richard ought to have apologized
at least. It was a week later, the last day of school,
when the note came in the mail. It was not written
on his office stationery this time, but on a square

piece of rag paper. It was polite, distant, and aloof. She read it till she had it by rote. "Dear Miss Talmadge: I wish to express my deep regret at the misunderstanding that occurred regarding your relationship with my brother. Sean joins with me in asking you to accept our sincere apologies for any inconvenience we caused you. We both wish you every success in your studies. Sincerely, Richard Bowden."

That was it. They had turned her life upside down, cost her her job and unmeasurable personal anguish. She had been chastised as a prostitute, all but raped, and this was called an "inconvenience," as though they had accidentally spilled a drink or stepped on her toe. With school over, she was inclined to leave the city to find work in another county for the summer. But organists seemed to be about as much in demand as flea trainers or lace makers.

She went around to talk to Vera and Jerry one day, and they had a different idea. "Come back and work for us," Vera said.

"Aye, we've hired a fellow who plays only six tunes—and those badly. That's all he knows. The same six tunes every night, till we're sick and tired of them," Jerry said.

"I don't know. You meet some strange people working in a club."

"You're thinking of that Bowden fellow," Vera said, reading her mind. "They don't come in any more, either of them. You never had but the one bad experience all the time you were here. Think about it. We'd be glad to have you back."

"We might sweeten the pot with an extra couple of quid a week," Jerry tempted. The absence of Laura was costing him considerably more, or at least he assumed the absence of some of his regular customers was due to her departure. Several of them had inquired after her.

Work was as difficult to find as she had always know it would be. She graduated with excellent grades, but still, if she didn't buy an organ and set up as a private instructor, she knew she wouldn't keep body and soul together. She was offered a position playing the organ in a department store to lure in customers, but it was what she called a toy organ. It all but played itself. It had rhythm sections and all manner of musical aids to make a beginner sound proficient.

In the end, she returned to the Chez Nous. Jerry even went to the expense of having her own cardboard likeness made for the window, but he might as well have saved his money. The creators managed to make it as ugly as the one of Aimée. Francis and Mavis, unaware of the extent of her difficulty with the Bowdens, didn't rail against her return to the club as she had feared they would. It was turning into summer weather, and though the club boasted air conditioning, it didn't turn it on high enough to prevent the fashion-conscious women from wearing their lightweight gowns. Wednesday and Thursday nights, Laura felt warm in the heavier outfits she had chosen for winter performances.

On Friday she went shopping and bought two new gowns. The black had always been the favorite of the customers, so she bought a daring black strapless, which would be worn mainly on Saturdays, the busiest night. The other was white chiffon over silk with narrow braided shoulder straps. It was this latter she chose for Friday's performance. She wanted a new hairstyle to go with it and leafed through magazines to select one. She piled her hair high on her head with loose curls playing about her ears. When Jerry's eyes swelled in admiration, she felt she had chosen well.

She was back in the groove, enjoying her work, and feeling particularly good on Friday with her new gown and hairdo. She stepped into the light, smiled, made her curtsy, and walked to the organ to begin "Mame," her upbeat opening number. She was familiar enough with it to cast her eyes around the room, calculating Jerry's probable profit from the evening. She saw a large table of clergymen, which would not please any of the staff. Church ministers did not drink the profitable liquor in any great quantity and were not heavy tippers. Their saving grace was that they would leave early to free the table for another party. The accents from a near table were American, always welcome since they ordered expensive dishes, much liquor, and tipped lavishly. They were also friendly and open in their manners. She smiled to see the waitress dancing attendance on them.

Then her eyes roved back to the farther recesses of the room, where the smaller tables held groups of two and four. Facial features could not be distinguished clearly, but one of the men had very much the outline of Richard Bowden. He was accompanied by a sophisticated blonde wearing a dark gown that covered one shoulder, leaving the other bare. Gemstones sparkled at her neck. She refused to look at that table again, in case it *was* Bowden. It probably isn't, she told herself, to quiet the jumping nerves. Why would he come here? He never wanted to see her again, and she wasn't seeing Sean, so that could not have brought him.

At the end of the first set, she was still uncertain whether it was Richard. She went back for her second half hour, and one of the waiters handed her a note with a five pound bill enclosed. She recognized the bold, black handwriting at once. It was his. "La Vie en Rose" was all that was written on the paper.

"Give the gentleman back his money, and tell him I don't take requests," she said.

"I can't say that! I told him you *do*. Crikey, Laura, he gave me a quid just to deliver the note, and you a fiver. You've *got* to do it."

"No, I don't. Give him back the money, and tell him I don't know that tune."

"You've played it before."

"Well, I don't play it now!" she said angrily, and resumed her playing.

The waiter gave her a sulky frown and returned to Bowden's table. Richard remained till he and his date had finished dinner, then left without any further attempt at communication.

She was livid with anger. Did he think a five pound note made up for the turmoil he had caused her? And not a single personal word on it, just the song title. She went to the kitchen and saw Roy, the waiter who had delivered the note, drinking a bottle of pop.

"How's the plutocrat?" Roy asked. "Too rich to play a tune for a fiver, eh? You must be daft."

"What did the man say?" she asked with an air of indifference.

"The man, namely Richard Bowden, said he was sorry to hear you no longer took requests. I didn't know who he was then. Jerry gave me the word. He's not too happy with you, my girl."

Jerry was not so unhappy as to actually berate her. The matter passed off without further comment.

On Saturday she cleaned her apartment, did her grocery shopping, had a hamburger at a corner shop with some student friends, and went back to her flat to shower and make ready for the night. At the club she wondered, as she slipped her new black gown over her head, whether Richard would come again. She also wondered who the woman with him had been. Laura wore her hair hanging loose and long that night. Jerry claimed he didn't know whether she was supposed to be an angel or a witch, but his smile showed that whichever it was, he approved.

"If the Bowden fellow and his lady should show up again, love, no need to offend them. He could bring us in the right sort of clientele. That was a genuine lady he was with last night. Vera saw their picture in the papers. Lady Althea Reidel, daughter of an earl. He bears no hard feelings about the fracas over his brother, so there's no reason for *you* to, is there?"

"I guess not," she agreed verbally, but of course Jerry and Vera knew only a part of the story. She had not revealed the whole extent of her insults to anyone.

She was nervous before going out to make her first curtsy. She had a strong feeling Richard would be there. That he had come with a lady showed her clearly he had no intention of pursuing her, but it still didn't explain why he had come at all. Her first cursory glance around the room didn't show any silhouette that resembled him. She first breathed a sigh of relief, then realized that the weight on her heart was disappointment. She kept such a sharp eye on the door that she failed to notice that the table closest to her was vacant. Not till Richard was being led to it did she see the two empty chairs and the white cloth set for one. Lady Althea was not along this time. She felt as nervous as a kitten. It was only the necessity of keeping her fingers moving that saved her from utter panic.

He sat down very calmly, without looking at her. He ordered wine and dinner and ate quietly, paying just as much attention to her as though he had never seen her before, and not a jot more. He didn't try to make any requests either through a waiter or directly. By the end of the second set he had finished his dinner. She was so on edge by then, she hoped he would leave. He was still there for the third set and the fourth, not saying anything, but looking at her more frequently than before, in a slow, intense way that made her lose her composure. When she rose to make her final curtsy, he too rose, but he left the restaurant and made no attempt to see her alone or to talk to her.

She was totally confused. Why was he doing this? She expected she might hear from him over the weekend, but there was no call, no knock at the door—nothing. All she saw of him was his picture in the tabloid with a smiling Lady Althea on his arm. They were attending a charity ball of which Lady Althea was one of the hostesses.

The next Friday he came to the Chez Nous alone again. It began to seem that he came only to disconcert or annoy her. She decided to do a little annoying of her own. She had determined never to sit with another customer in her life, though she often received invitations. On Friday she changed her mind. A traveling salesman from the provinces sat alone, watching her. He was in his forties, a harmless-looking man, rather handsome in a second-rate way. In an effort to appear youthful, he wore his hair longer than became one of his years. His tailoring also was too youthful to suit his incipient paunch. His main attraction was that his table was close to Richard's. When the man came up to the organ to request a number, he also asked her to join him for a drink.

She could smell the liquor on his breath, but men *did* drink at the club, so that was not surprising. "All right, but just one drink," she replied, smiling, and went with him to his table.

From the corner of her eye she saw a glimpse of Richard's stiff, disapproving, and thoroughly start-led face glowering at her as she passed, without acknowledging his presence.

"What will it be for the little lady?" the man asked in a loud, common voice, with a proud look around to see what the customers thought of his having walked off with the prize.

"A glass of red wine for me, please," she answered quietly.

"Let's make it champagne," the man said. "I've just closed a very profitable deal in the city. McLaughlin's the name—hardware's the game. Ernest McLaughlin, from Reading. You may have heard of the McLaughlin Hardware Stores? I own half a dozen of them, spread from Reading to London. I've just tied up an exclusive dealership in Belter's line of tools. The only store that handles them within a hundred-mile radius. I'm celebrating, miss. What's your name, then?"

"Laura," she answered, wishing he would not shout quite so loudly across the table.

"That's a nice name. We'll share a bottle of the old bubbly, what?"

"If you like," she agreed.

He hollered for a waiter to bring a bottle of the best and hang the expense. He laughed clamorously when the cork escaped the waiter's fingers to land in the middle of the table.

"Drink up!" he ordered jovially.

"To your continued success," she said, lifting her glass. She noticed his fingers trembled when he took up his own glass and soon learned that he was feeling the effects of his celebration.

"I'll drink to that. I may open up another pair of shops. Newbury doesn't have what *I* would call a real hardware shop, nor does Chesham. Oh, there's money in hardware, miss. Don't let anyone tell you otherwise."

"That's nice," she said, trying to think of some quiet topic to pass ten minutes. She would quickly drink her champagne and disappear.

"Aye, I'm sure it would please you," he said with a knowing wink, his eyes scanning her shoulders and bosom.

"I'm happy for *you* is what I meant," she said, her smile thinning.

"You know how to pick them, miss. I daresay a girl like yourself can spot a bulging wallet a room away. There's plenty in mine tonight," he told her, patting his breast pocket, which presumably contained the full wallet.

She said nothing, but took a gulp of the champagne to hurry her escape. He began a series of exaggerated compliments on her appearance, comparing her to Marilyn Monroe and other unlikely screen beauties. "I said to myself the minute you made your bows, there's the one for you tonight, Ernest, my boy."

She put down her glass and prepared to leave.
"Thank you so much for the champagne. It was
lovely," she said.

His hand reached out and clamped her wrist. "Not
so fast, miss. What time do you get out of here?"

"I have to go now," she said, pulling her wrist
away. His fingers clenched it harder.

"You haven't answered my question."

"Let go," she said in a low, angry whisper.

"Not till we come to terms," he parried in no low
voice.

She looked fearfully around for a waiter. A black
shoulder suddenly loomed up behind her. "The lady
wishes to leave now," Richard said in a commanding
tone.

"Who might *you* be, mister?" McLaughlin asked
in a voice of contempt.

"I'm the fellow who is going to break your nose in
about ten seconds," Richard threatened.

McLaughlin shoved his chair back, and rose to his
feet, flinging Laura aside. She bumped against a
chair and grabbed it to steady herself, aware of the
customers' curious glances, the ripple of excited
exclamations, aware most of all of the lethal sparkle
in Richard's eyes. He looked like a wild animal,
poised to strike.

"We'll see about that!" the hardware merchant
proclaimed, and drew his arm back to deliver a
glancing blow to Richard's chin. It bounced his head
back but did no serious damage except to raise the
victim's temper to an alarming degree.

While Laura watched in mute chagrin, Richard
recovered and landed a neat right to Mr.
McLaughlin's nose. Blood trickled down his face,

causing two younger gentlemen at the next table to rise hastily and pull at Bowden's arms, already raised for more battle.

"Get your hands off me!" Richard growled.

"If you want a brawl, mate, try somebody your own age," the younger of the interlopers taunted. Richard was angry enough to do just that. He let fly his fist and sent the man reeling against the next table. Suddenly pandemonium broke out as the ladies squealed, and their men rose to their feet to protect them. One venturesome lady clambered up on her chair to gain a better view of the goings-on.

An ill-advised new waiter ran into the street and hailed down a passing police car. Within two minutes the police were in the room, dragging away Mr. Bowden and Ernest McLaughlin and asking pertinent questions of the customers. Laura too was hauled off to the station with the men, while Jerry wrung his hands and told Vera that both McLaughlin and Bowden had left without settling their accounts, and if Laura Talmadge thought she was going to get paid for this night's work, she had another thing coming. He'd dock her for the two meals.

"Well, I never!" Vera sighed. "Here we thought that Bowden was a *gentleman,* and he's nothing but a common brawler when all's said and done."

Richard had recovered to a state of indignant, hostile civility by the time he faced the reporting officer at the station. As McLaughlin had struck the first blow, it was for Richard to lay charges, which he generously declined to do. They were all three dismissed with a warning, which Laura hoped was the end of it.

"I'll take you home in a cab," Richard told her. "I

left my car at the club." His eyes were blazing. He could not say much in front of the constable, but she had no desire to be alone with him.

"*I'll* be taking the young lady home," McLaughlin told him, which caused Laura to grab on to Richard's arm rather quickly and hurry out of the station with him. He hailed the first cab that cruised by and shoved her into the back seat more brusquely than was really necessary.

"I hope you're satisfied with your night's work" were the first angry words he spoke when they were alone.

"There wouldn't have been any fracas if *you* hadn't interfered. I was just leaving."

"Your hardware merchant had other ideas. The fracas might better have been avoided by your refusing to accept the hospitality of a vulgar, dissolute inebriated bum. What did you expect when you agreed to join him?"

"I certainly didn't expect *you* to beat the poor man up and get us all arrested! Why don't you mind your own business."

"That's gratitude for you!"

"What were you doing at the club anyway? I had hoped, when you said you never wanted to see me again, that you would never come back. The Chez Nous is an odd place for you to go *not* to see me."

"Don't flatter yourself my going had anything to do with *you.*"

"Perhaps you're going to make a movie about it, starring that plain-faced cow you had with you the other time."

"For your information, my guest was *Lady* Althea Reidel, and she is not a *cow.*"

"She's certainly no heifer. A little mature for most men's taste, I think."

"I doubt your hardware merchant would approve of her, but then he obviously prefers the *common* touch that you inevitably supply."

"I never made any claim to be a lady, and if *you* are a typical specimen of English gentleman, I prefer the common touch, thank you very much."

"Lady Althea was right," he said with a sneer, then looked to see if she meant to inquire for Lady Althea's words. When she did not, he told her anyway. "A pretty face, but unfortunately the girl lacks breeding."

"Please return my compliments to your aging friend. Full of breeding, but unfortunately, the lady lacks a pretty face. Which would she *really* prefer to have, I wonder."

"They are not mutually exclusive. In *my* opinion, she has both."

"I wonder you could tear yourself away from the paragon for so many nights."

"I went from a sense of duty, if you must know. I wouldn't want you to get the idea I was hanging about hoping for a crumb of your attention. You complained to Sean that I had caused you to lose your job. I was only doing my small bit to show the proprietor of the club that I bore it no ill will—no customers would be lost on *my* account, if he chose to reinstate you."

"One visit would have been sufficient to establish your good will."

The cab pulled up to her doorway as he finished speaking. "Furthermore, you ought to move out of this *slum,"* he added.

"I've made application for a suite at Buckingham Palace. I expect to be moving in any day now," she answered blandly.

He got out and held the door for her, then turned to pay the driver. "You'd better keep him," she said, noticing what he was doing.

"I am seeing you up to your apartment."

"I know the way. Thanks for the lift."

"There is something I'd like to say to you in private," he told her, still angry.

"I don't much care for the way you behave in private, Mr. Bowden. Much too *gentlemanly* to suit *me*. Furthermore, I haven't the least interest in anything you have to say. Good night." She turned and sped to her door, upstairs and in, locking it behind her. She was shaking from the ordeal.

Why had she ever agreed to sit with that cursed hardware merchant? She had done it to make Richard jealous—that was the sum total of it. But instead of making him jealous, she had given him an even worse opinion of her. She may have convinced him once she was not what he thought, but this night's folly had surely reversed the opinion. "The girl lacks breeding." She felt a strong desire to put her underbred fingers around Lady Reidel's neck and strangle her. How *dare* they sit in judgment of her? He had brought that woman to the club to *laugh* at her.

The newspaper photo of Richard and Lady Althea had been cut out and lay on her coffee table within easy reach. She had looked at it several times a day, comparing her own face and body to that of the chosen lady. Lady Althea was not beautiful, but she certainly had a regal set to her head and a haughty, condescending smile. Now she crumpled up the picture and threw it into the wastebasket.

Jerry, at a high tide of displeasure with her, phoned and advised her that her services would no longer be required if she didn't learn how to behave herself.

"It's not my fault. You can't fire me—I quit!" she protested, and slammed down the receiver.

He phoned right back to say she wouldn't be receiving her last week's wages, as there were two meals to be paid for. "Send Bowden the bill. He can afford it. If I don't get my money, I'll sue."

The next morning's tabloids, more interested in scandal than veracity, carried a two-inch banner headline about the affair. "Prominent Industrialist Bowden in Barroom Brawl over Blonde" was smeared across the top of the sheet. There was a two-year-old photo of Richard shaking hands with the prime minister at the opening of some factory with a woman who looked very much like Princess Margaret Rose in the background. Next to it was a reproduction of the cheap cardboard effigy of her that graced the window of the Chez Nous. She groaned to think of the embarrassment this would cause Richard. The account of the incident was similarly sensational, making the whole thing even more sleazy than it actually was—and it was bad enough.

They had statements from waitresses and customers of the club, taken out of context, implying that Bowden kept a nightly vigil at the club, hoping for a kind word from the entertainer. Her own name did not appear as often as that of Richard. She was more usually referred to as "The Blonde." It also mentioned Sir Greville Bowden and Hazelhurst. Even the name of Lady Althea was there, outlining her "friendship" with Bowden. If fate had set out to make Richard despise her and her lack of breeding, it could not have done a better job.

It was her next-door neighbor who brought the tabloid to her attention. "What luck!" the woman crowed. "This could be the making of you, Laura. I bet you could get into the movies or on the telly with this kind of free publicity. You could sell your story like the girls in the Profumo affair. "The Bowden Affair" they'd call it. Coo, how lovely!"

"Oh, my God!" Laura gasped, horrified to be placed in such racy company.

"That Richard Bowden isn't half bad-looking. I quite fancied him myself."

"When did you meet him?" Laura asked, startled.

"The day you went to the wedding with the other young fellow. He came knocking on my door, asking if I'd seen you. I tried to lure him in to stay a spell, but he was in such a hurry to be after you he didn't half listen to me. I knew then you had him locked up tight. He was crazed with worry. He never did accept my invitation to come back."

Laura winced to think what impression this brazen trollop had made on Richard. No wonder he'd suggested she move out. The place was little better than a bawdy house. Why should he think she was any different from her neighbors? And how could she possibly move, with flats as scarce as hen's teeth and impossibly expensive.

She took the tabloid to Francis and Mavis, knowing they would see it sooner or later and wanting them to hear her version. "Maybe I shouldn't play the church organ, Francis. The story sounds so immoral, though it wasn't really."

"It'll blow over," he calmed her. "Just go on as usual, and if anyone mentions it, I'll explain it away."

"I don't see much disgrace in it for *you,* Laura," Mavis pointed out. "It's this Bowden who looks a proper fool. I'll bet *he's* blushing today in front of all his friends."

"I'm afraid it will attract undesirable elements to my flat," she mentioned.

"Your address isn't given, and your phone number isn't in the book, so I don't see how it can," Mavis comforted.

"That's true. I'll sit tight and see what happens."

"If things get rough, you can always come back here for a while," Mavis assured her.

She spent the Sunday with her brother's family, discussing what other job she might find.

"The only other offer I had was to demonstrate organs in a department store," she told them sadly. She knew other jobs like the one she'd just lost would be open after her new infamy, but had no intention of resuming that career.

"Take it then, till something else comes along," Francis advised. "You've got to earn a living."

"I'll start pounding the pavement on Monday," she decided, and the subject was dropped.

It was a peaceful and pleasant Sunday with the baby cooing and beginning to sit up and smile. Laura knew that Mavis sometimes envied her her career and even her looks. She often mentioned such things, but on that day it was Mavis who was envied. Laura wondered if she would ever be so happily

settled as her brother and his wife were. It didn't
take much to make them happy—just a small cot-
tage, each other, Francis's job, and the baby.

When she went to the store that had made her an
offer, she found that the position had been filled.
She picked up the papers to search the classified ads
and went back to her flat. There was one similar
advertisement for another shop. She called and got
an interview for that same afternoon. Before getting
ready to go to it, she decided to have lunch. Eating
at home would save precious money, which was in
short supply now, till she landed a job. She fried
bacon and eggs and ate them in the living room while
she watched the noon news. To keep her good suit
clean, she changed into jeans and a T-shirt. The shirt
was one popular with the Academy students. It
showed Beethoven and Bach having a glass of beer.
'Beer, Bach and Beethoven—the Three B's' it said.

When there was a knock at the door, she had no
premonition that it was a Bowden. She knew that
newspaper headlines would keep Richard miles from
her. It would be Francis or one of her school mates.

She went to unlock the door and found herself
regarding Lady Althea Reidel. The woman had
draped herself in a set of sable skins for an afternoon
visit. Her dark blond hair was as smooth as silk.
There was literally not one hair out of place. It had
been heavily lacquered with spray. Her face, too,
was painted as perfectly as a picture. She wore a
well-cut caramel-colored suit, tan pigskin gloves,
nylons, and pumps. There was about her the staid
appearance of a royal princess, someone who must
always be well-groomed but never in any way out-
standing. Classic understatement was her theme.
Laura saw at close range that the woman wasn't

really as old as she had thought from the picture and the club. It was her general bearing that misled one from a distance.

"I am Lady Althea Reidel. May I come in?" she asked, then brushed past Laura without awaiting permission.

She slowly looked all about the room, her nose quivering in distaste at the dirty dishes on the sofa table and the poor decorating taste in evidence everywhere. Finally, she regarded Laura. Her first expression of distaste hardened to acute dislike.

"I see you are a music lover," she said, and laughed as her eyes skimmed the T-shirt. "Richard mentioned your interest in it."

Laura found speech impossible. She had to suppress her mirth at the woman's accent, so cultivated it sounded like a parody of the queen. "I think you know why I am here?" Lady Althea asked.

Laura knew the visit was connected in some way with Richard. If he had sent this harpy to *spy* on her or to give her a lecture, it was more than the human heart could bear. For curiosity's sake, however, she did not show her the door. "I presume it is a social call?" Laura answered with lofty grace. "Do have a seat, Lady Althea. Tea?" she asked, plumping herself down before the cold pot.

"Thank you, no," the lady replied, perching on the very outer edge of the sofa after first glancing to see it was not likely to dirty her skirt.

"Actually, I have come about your . . . association with Sean Bowden," she said, choosing her words with care.

"Really? I thought it more likely it was my . . . association with Richard that brought you. He tells me you two are friends."

"Both of them. It is all one and the same thing, isn't it? Richard only sees you to encourage you to break off with his brother."

"Is *that* what he tells you?" she asked, and laughed lightly. "But I broke off with Sean ages ago. As soon as I met Richard, in fact," she added, leading her on.

"Yes, I was afraid—I thought that might be the way things stood. Men are such fools, are they not?"

"Utter morons," Laura agreed, her smile brittle.

"Richard has reached that age where it is expected he will marry soon. He is heir to Hazelhurst and the baronetcy, but of course you know that."

"Of course."

"One feels he ought to marry and produce the next heir."

"Quite like a Victorian novel," Laura said, while listening with amused interest.

"Not quite. The family history predates Victoria by several centuries." Lady Althea added hastily and humorlessly. "Theirs is one of the old, aristocratic English families, like my own. Richard's wife must be of that class. One has to be so very careful. There are duties incumbent on the wife of a baronet —things you would know nothing about."

"One is eager to hear," Laura egged her on. "What is expected of Lady Richard?"

"Lady Richard? My dear, you mean Lady Bowden! A baronet's wife uses her husband's last name."

"Fancy that! Richard is always telling me how educational a second language is. I really must get busy and learn to speak Court English."

"Lady Bowden has traditionally been one of the ladies-in-waiting to Her Majesty. Appearing at court functions, arranging debuts and balls, sponsoring charitable organizations—all these will be expected of Richard's wife. Now that his business interests have gone international, there will be other work-related social duties as well. Visiting guests and dignitaries to entertain at Hazelhurst, trips abroad, and so on. Lady Bowden must be multilingual and have some familiarity with customs abroad."

"I adored Italy," Laura threw in, when Lady Althea stopped to draw breath.

"She must be aware of all the minutiae governing large social gatherings—protocol. You must see the necessity for his marrying the right woman."

"And do you feel Richard is not aware of this?" Laura asked, batting her lashes and playing the innocent. How bold and forward this woman was, to come barging in, warning her away from Richard! She would sit still for no more insults from the high and mighty.

"You know how men are. They will ofttimes be led by their hearts, led into folly they soon learn to regret. That *scandal* last week—it did his career great harm."

"Did Richard send you here?" Laura asked bluntly.

"I am here on behalf of the whole family. Sir Greville, Lady Bowden—you cannot know the heartbreak you are causing them. Sir Greville's not at all well, either. Marriage with Richard would be a disaster for him and for you. You would be very much out of place in their world, Miss Talmadge. Give it up," Lady Althea urged, leaning forward to emphasize her request or rather demand. It was hard to determine from her proud, guarded face whether she was pleading or ordering.

"You plan to fill this multifaceted role yourself, I take it?"

"My background suits me for it."

"One thing is lacking, Lady Althea. Common sense. I wouldn't marry Richard Bowden if he begged me on bended knee."

"He *has* asked you then!" the woman exclaimed.

"Oh, is *that* why you came, to snoop for information? Why didn't you just ask Richard? Would you excuse me now? I have to take out the garbage. So kind of you to drop around. Do call again whenever you happen to be in the neighborhood. You can catch a bus uptown at the corner."

"My chauffeur is waiting," Lady Althea countered, rising sedately to gather up gloves and purse. "May I assure Sir Greville and Lady Bowden that you will act properly in the matter?"

"I always act properly, ma'am," Laura answered unhelpfully.

"I mean you will not marry Richard?"

"Not at all, if Sir Greville and Lady Bowden really have any interest in it. More importantly, you may put your own fears to rest. I wouldn't dream of marrying him . . . unless he asks me again," she added, to worry the interfering woman.

"Again?"

"Just between us ladies, Lady Althea, you know how hard it is to nab a rich fellow. And I *would* love to be lady-in-waiting to Her Majesty." She hastened the astonished woman to the door as she spoke, pushed her out, and locked it.

Her heart was pounding with annoyance. The *gall* of the old crow to come lording it over her, with her *one's* and her *ladies-in-waiting*. She didn't think Richard had sent her, either, though it was entirely possible his parents had. She darted to the window to see Lady Althea enter a Rolls-Royce of burnished silver. A uniformed chauffeur closed the door after her like the liveried footman of yore.

After her anger simmered down, she had to admit there was some truth in the argument presented. She would make a perfectly terrible wife for a man in Richard's position. But as the matter was purely academic, she tried to put it out of her mind and get ready for the interview.

The manager of the store was either not aware of Laura's notoriety or willing to overlook it since she was pretty enough to draw in customers by her presence. The salary was small, and to make her finances tighter she soon had a call from Jerry, bumping up her rent. Its former low price had been due to her being his employee. Now, when she returned from work at night, tired and dispirited, she had the unenviable chore of trying to find a different flat. For a week she went from address to address only to find the place already taken or the rent too high or the accommodation utterly unsuitable. In the end she paid Jerry's higher price and took lessons in the evenings at the store to augment her income. Customers buying a new organ often wanted a few sessions to learn which knobs to pull to bring forth the desired sounds. Really, there wasn't much more to it than that. The chords played automatically, and a one-finger right hand was built up electronically to sound like three notes. They would have been smarter to simply buy a record player, but they would tell her they wanted to "really learn to play." She sighed to think of the years it had taken her, and they were coming to seem like wasted years too. No one wanted a concert organist.

To keep her technique up and to work on the foot pedals that hardly existed in the department store machines, she went twice a week to her brother's church organ. Alone in the loft with the rich music filling the empty church, she felt some sense of peace. It was impossible not to think of her cousin Anne's wedding day, and the fiasco surrounding her own part in it. She wondered what had happened to Sean and looked for Richard's name or face in the newspapers, but did not see either one. They had dropped out of her life as suddenly as they had dropped in, leaving no trace but the lonely ache in her heart and an overwhelming sense of loss.

No movie or television man came hunting her down after her brief brush with fame, and there were no offers to print her story. She was thankful to be anonymous but did wish she could make enough money to afford a better apartment. On the other hand she thought, and hated herself for even thinking it, how would anyone from the past find her if she moved? In her heart she knew there was only one person she wanted to come seeking her out, and he didn't come. At least she didn't read in the papers that he had become engaged to Lady Althea Reidel, which was a small blessing.

Chapter Eight

It was on a Friday afternoon in late June that she saw Richard again. He came into the music department of the store just after four, looking out of place in his business suit. Most of the customers wore shirt sleeves in the summer. She realized her memory of him had faded. He looked taller, more handsome, more *alive* than she had been remembering him. She thought he hadn't seen her, since he spoke to the manager, obviously on business. He never once looked towards her corner, but after five or ten minutes the manager led him towards her.

"Miss Talmadge, will you look after this gentleman?" he said with a happy twinkle in his eyes. Her boss only wore that particular twinkle when he had a good sale in view. It was hard to conceive that Richard was about to buy an organ. In her association with him and Sean, neither of them had mentioned playing it or knowing anyone who did.

"Miss Talmadge is our expert," he advised Richard. "She'll be able to assist you. I know very little about the larger organs you are interested in. Miss Talmadge calls these you see here *toys*," he added with a laugh. "The gentleman is interested in a console model," he told Laura. "It's for church use. He wants one without the automatic rhythm section and all that. A full complement of foot pedals and a stylish cabinet that will suit a church."

She saw Richard regarding her unconcernedly, with perhaps just a shadow of wariness deep in his eyes. They were to pretend no previous acquaintance, it seemed.

"You know we don't have anything like that in stock, Mr. Peters," she said. "There's virtually no demand for them. If it's a church organ Mr.—the gentleman wants, he would do better to go to—"

"We can *order* one," Peters told her sharply, for he wasn't happy to lose out on a good sale.

"If you aren't in a hurry, we can," she agreed.

"There's no mad panic. It's a bequest to our local church by my family," Richard explained.

"That's a mighty fine gesture," Mr. Peters complimented.

Laura considered his speech. It was generous certainly, but she doubted his desire for a church organ had brought him to this out-of-the-way department store. His local church organist could have directed him to a likelier spot.

She stood uncertainly, looking to Mr. Peters for a clue as to what she ought to do. "Get out the catalogues," he said impatiently. "Show Mr. Bowden what we have—can order, that is to say.

We'll put through a special order. There's no reason we couldn't have it within the week. Would a week be soon enough for you, sir?"

"A week would be fine. Shall we see the catalogues now?" he added, looking to Laura.

"Use my desk," Peters offered magnanimously.

She led Richard to the desk, not a private office, but a desk in the corner of the store with a chair behind it and another in front. She'd been working since noon. She knew her lipstick had worn off, her hair was no longer tidy, and her dress, a simple, tailored cotton suitable to a shopgirl, no longer fresh. She swallowed nervously as she rifled the desk drawers for the catalogues.

"I'll just move this chair out here where we can both look at the catalogues," Richard said very much in his normal voice, but when he placed the chairs, she thought he was trying to get them at an angle that would cut off Peters's view of them.

She laid the three catalogues on the desk top, and began to glance through them. "How much did you intend to spend?" she asked.

"I have no idea what an organ costs. We want something fine, large enough to fill a medium-sized church. The music I mean, not the organ," he added quickly, and smiled. He seemed a little nervous, which surprised her. No boast of being rich today. "Something like your brother has at St. Peter's," he added.

"That's a very old organ, a pipe organ. It's no longer made," she replied.

"It has a beautiful tone still."

When had he heard it? And if he had heard it, he'd heard her play, for no one else played at St. Peter's. Had he gone to the church only to hear her?

"Yes, it has," she replied, trying not to flush. "This is about the size you want, I think," she went on, pointing to a picture in the catalogue. "It has a separate set of speakers. The organs nowadays are all electronic. The old pipe organs are practically obsolete. The sound is still rich on the new ones, though. I've played one like this at the Academy."

"I understand the store gives a set of lessons as well," he mentioned.

"Yes."

"Are you the instructress?"

"Yes, but I doubt your church organist will require lessons. They're only given here in the shop. We don't go out of the department store."

"Our organist can come in, to be shown the fine points."

"That can be easily arranged. Hammond has a nice console as well. You won't want to buy such an expensive item without making some comparisons," she said, taking up another book, proud of her composure.

He leaned a little closer over her shoulder. She felt the brush of his shoulder against hers, and smelled the spicy scent of his shaving lotion, which brought back such poignant memories. But as soon as he touched her, he pulled away and straightened up as though he had been pulled on a string. They looked through the catalogues for a quarter of an hour, the talk strictly business right till the end when he risked a more personal comment.

"I see you no longer play at the club," he said casually, while she flipped pages, looking for possible alternatives for him.

"No, I don't."

"Were you fired, or did you quit?"

"It depends on who is telling the story. In my opinion I quit."

"You're better off away from that place. Do you make a decent living here?"

"Again, it is a matter of opinion. *You* wouldn't find it decent, but it keeps me out of the poorhouse. I get by."

"You play so beautifully; why don't you pursue a concert career?" Richard continued, oblivious to her discomfort.

"There isn't much of an audience for organ music," she replied shortly.

"Yes, I remember the sparse crowd Hans Grebel drew. It seems a shame—all your hard work wasted."

"It wasn't wasted. I enjoy it. How is Sean?" she ventured, her curiosity getting the better of her, since he had led the way onto personal ground himself.

"Some movie mogul convinced him he'll go farther in the business if he has a degree. He passed his year and is returning in the autumn. For the summer he is a handyman at Pinewood Studios. At least he's in show business, he says. He's currently in love with a Eurasian girl, a starlet, who has some small part in the film there. I shan't be so foolish as to interfere this time."

It was an ambiguous comment. Did he mean he wouldn't risk further ignominy to himself, or was it a sort of apology? She looked up at him, but his eyes were turned to the page, so she learned nothing further.

"It's nearly time for me to leave," she said. "Do

you want to think about the organs we've been looking at and decide later?"

"Which do *you* like?"

"The Hammond is my personal favorite, but this one is a better bargain for your money," she said, pointing to another booklet.

"I'll take the Hammond," he said. She looked at him, a question in her eyes. "You know a good deal more about organs than I do. I'll take your advice," he said, making it clear it was her professional opinion that had guided him and not a personal preference.

Mr. Peters ambled up to the desk. "How are we coming along?" he asked. "You've got Mr. Bowden stuck off in a dark corner, Miss Talmadge. What, you're only showing him three catalogues? There are half a dozen more behind the counter!" He turned to Bowden to add, "It is impossible to find decent help nowadays."

"Miss Talmadge has been very helpful," Richard said quickly. "I particularly asked to see the Hammond book. You are fortunate to have someone so knowledgeable working for you. And you recommend the Hammond then, Miss Talmadge?"

"It's a fine organ," she agreed.

"Good, I'll take it."

"I'll just write up the order for you," Peters said, smiling fondly at the price listed. When the sale amounted to five figures, it was Peters himself who wrote up the bill.

Laura went to comb her hair and freshen her lipstick before leaving. She took her time, thinking the bill would have been written by the time she was ready to leave. The idea had taken root that Richard

had really come to see her. Of course he *did* want to
buy an organ, but there were many stores closer to
his office that sold them. She felt he would probably
offer her a ride home. She hardly dared to think
what would come of it, but was hopeful about a
reconciliation.

"I'm leaving now, Mr. Peters," she said on her
way out.

"See you tomorrow," Peters answered, still smiling.

"Thank you for your help," Richard said, then
turned back to chat with Peters.

She felt conceit had gotten the better of her. He
hadn't come to see her at all. He was probably
unhappy and embarrassed when he saw her there,
but was too gentlemanly to walk out. He'd treated
the situation well, she admitted, and was more
furious with him than ever.

On Saturday morning, she asked Mr. Peters
whether the deal for the organ had been completed
satisfactorily. "Signed, sealed, and to be delivered
next Friday afternoon," he told her. "You're to go
down to the church in Sussex and see that it's
working properly. It is to be delivered there. I told
Bowden you would do it—on company time, of
course. It will be a bit of a break from the shop for
you."

"Did he ask me to go?" she inquired.

"Yes, in fact, he's to pick you up here at three and
take you down himself. He's wonderfully interested
in organs, Mr. Bowden. I have some hope of selling
him one of our toy organs for himself. He said he
might drop in this week and try one out. He is a
great organ enthusiast. Knows all the spots in Lon-

don where you might hear one. You would probably
know the places he was talking about. They meant
nothing to me."

"What places did he mention?" she asked with
interest.

"Some little church or other—St. Peter's, I think it
was. He tells me they have a dandy organist who
plays on Sundays. He's a fine gentleman. I wish
there were more like him, buying up organs for their
church. See what that fellow wants," he added, as a
customer strolled in to play with the toys.

Richard didn't come in to look at the smaller
organs during the week. Knowing he was going to be
in the store on Friday to take her to Sussex with him,
she took some pains with her appearance on that
special day. She was determined to look not only
attractive but eminently respectable. She couldn't
hope to match Lady Althea in elegance, but she
chose a light-blue tailored dress with a white collar
and white piping down the front. Her trim figure
added a note of fashion to the staid ensemble, as did
her hair, coiled into a fashionable knot at the back.
Lest she look too much like a schoolteacher, she
wore high-heeled sandals. They were too uncomfortable for the store, but she'd put them on after lunch
for the drive.

A trip to Sussex begun at three was not likely to
see her home before dinner. She wondered what
plans Richard had made, and whether this hour had
been only convenient to himself with no thought of
her at all. She was nervous as three drew near. She
went to tidy her hair and refresh her makeup. When
she came out of the powder room at five to three, he
was in the shop, talking to Mr. Peters. He looked up
and smiled at her in a way that tugged at her

heartstrings. It was a fond, wistful *intimate* smile, more telling than words.

"Here she is, all set to take off," Peters said jovially. "The organ should be there at the church waiting for you. Miss Talmadge will make sure it is in prime shape, all the stops working, and all that. If there is any trouble, Miss Talmadge, let me know, and I'll get after the company."

"I will. Are you ready, Mr. Bowden?"

"Ready and waiting," he said with an effort at ease, but she sensed some agitation in him.

He had his car parked across the street illegally. "You're lucky you didn't get a ticket," she told him.

"I speak French and they back off, remember?" he answered, holding the door open for her. "I hope my luck holds."

"They're not likely to give you a ticket after you've left," she pointed out.

"True, but that wasn't what I meant," he said, inserting the key and starting the engine.

After they had pulled away from the curb, the traffic was dense enough to inhibit any real conversation. Till they were beyond the city on a western route heading to Hazelhurst, there was no talk of any consequence.

"How far is it?" she asked.

"Sixty-odd miles as the crow flies. Too bad we're not crows. How long does it take you to check out an organ?"

"I've never had the privilege of checking out such a large one. It depends on whether there's anything wrong with it too. We usually try out the toys at the shop, and if there's any trouble, the technician goes to the house to fix it. That way he can fix up anything additional that goes awry during transportation. I really don't know why I was sent. I don't know a thing about electronics."

"You know how the organ should sound, though."

"Yes, I suppose I can give your church organist a few tips on the various pulls, that sort of thing. Who is he, by the way?"

"His name's Everett."

"Has he been playing long?"

"He's only learning. Our old organist died. Mr. Everett's been taking lessons for six months."

"I doubt he'll be able to get the maximum performance from what you bought, then. But he should grow into it eventually, if he's serious."

They discussed the organ for a few moments, then he asked suddenly, "Is there some particular hour you have to be back in London? Do you have a date, or . . ."

"Not tonight," she answered. "When does the train leave?"

"Train? I have no idea. It won't be necessary for you to take the train back. I have to return to London this evening myself. I have a meeting tomorrow morning—a board meeting. I'll drive you."

"That's very convenient. Thanks," she said, reading no special tribute to herself into the arrangement.

"I'm the one who should be thanking you for coming."

"It's my job," she answered, then turned to gaze out the window and remark on how the cities were encroaching upon each other, till soon there would be no countryside left unpaved.

"Except Kew Gardens," he reminded her. "Do you like the country?"

"I grew up in the country. I love it."

"Hazelhurst is countrified. It's close to a village, but with no developments nearby. It's like going back a hundred years, to step out the door. If a plane doesn't swoop past or a motorcycle roar by, you might think you were in a Constable painting."

"It was like that where I used to live," she told him. "When I first moved to London, I couldn't believe the noise and traffic."

They chatted easily, exchanging youthful reminiscences. It didn't seem odd to be telling him about the Welsh pony she and Francis had owned and the little cart her father had attached to it for them. They also competed with tales of exploits of dogs, bicycles, Christmas family traditions, and all sorts of things.

In the late afternoon, the car pulled up in front of the church. It wasn't a large edifice, but it was beautiful, its structure early Gothic, built before the flamboyant style had caught on. Clean ogee windows swept skywards. There was a single row of gargoyles in front and small flying buttresses on the sides, overgrown with ivy to soften the sharp lines.

"How lovely!" she exclaimed, admiring it.

"If Mr. Peters is as good as his word, the organ should be in the loft by now."

"Are we meeting Mr. Everett here?" she asked.

"He should be here soon. He works in the village. He's coming as soon as he can."

This sounded a fairly haphazard arrangement, but she went into the vestibule with him, inevitably reminded of that other encounter in a church vestibule. He said nothing but opened the door to the loft and followed her up the dark steps. "We really need a light here," he said prosaically.

The new organ sat in state in the center of the choir loft. She was eager to sit down at it, to try its paces. "I didn't bring any music! How stupid of me!" she exclaimed. "I hope there's some in the church."

"Yes, I have a few of our popular hymns here," he answered, opening an age-yellowed book, its pages dog-eared by time and usage.

She set the stops she wanted and took up a book. It was a delight to have a brand new organ to play, after those well-worn items the Academy provided. The walnut wood gleamed like dark honey in the shafts of the setting sun. She played two selections while Richard stood silent, watching her, listening.

"It appears to have come through transportation in perfect shape," she declared.

"What?" he asked, shaking himself to attention.

She repeated her opinion. "Excellent. My luck holds," he said.

Mr. Everett suddenly appeared beside them. He was an office clerk, a man in his early thirties with dark hair and a tanned face.

"She's a whopper. I doubt I'll be able to handle this one, Mr. Bowden," he said fearfully. "Our old organ was as much as I could handle. I see you have got my three hymns opened for me. I'll give them a try."

The man was a barely competent musician. He played the proper notes but without feeling or joy. He made no variation from the stops she had set, and worst of all, used no foot pedals to augment the bass tones. She looked at Richard, amazed that he had purchased such an extravagant organ for so untalented a man.

"I'll come over on the weekend and practice," Mr. Everett said when he had finished his three tunes. "I have a cricket match tonight. I must get home to dinner." He said his good-byes and left.

"Shall we head back to town?" Laura asked.

"Not if my luck holds. I had hoped you would join me for dinner," he said, his expression showing concern for her answer.

She felt a sense of elation. "It is getting a little late. Let's have a bite before we leave," she agreed.

"Yes, Mother is expecting us," he said, throwing her into a spasm of alarm.

Chapter Nine

She had a frightening image of a *grande dame,* similar to Lady Althea but older, sitting at a giant table surrounded by footmen. Laura was certain she'd spill her soup or use the wrong silver or say the wrong thing. And after that wretched tabloid spread, she just couldn't face his parents. "I—I'm not very hungry, Richard," she said tentatively, wishing to get out of it.

"You don't have to eat much. A bite, as you said."

"Couldn't we stop for a hamburger on the way back?"

"I told Mother we would dine at Hazelhurst."

"Oh, dear, with your whole family?" she asked, aghast.

"Sean is at work in London, and my father isn't well. He's bedridden. It'll be only my mother and myself. Nothing formal."

When he saw her obviously frightened half to death, he continued gently, "I told Mother we'd be there. She'd like to meet you. She's very much interested in organ music," he added, "and alone so much I thought your visit would be a pleasant diversion for her." But she knew instinctively his mother's diversion had little if anything to do with it. He wanted to see if she could fit into his milieu, and it frightened her to even consider it.

The awful image of a noble *dame* dwindled to more manageable proportions, but still she wasn't eager. "But she's a *lady!* Lady Bowden. I—I've never . . ." She stopped, embarrassed by her own childish babble. "If you've told her we're coming, then I must," she decided, but still with great reluctance.

"Don't be frightened of the handle. She's not at all of the old school. Her friends call her Tally-ho Bowden, to give you an idea of her informality."

"What a strange thing to call her."

Nevertheless, she looked extremely forbidding to Laura, when she was eventually presented to her. Or perhaps it was the drive through the acres of park land, up a twisting graveled path to a veritable castle, that upset her nerves. She'd often thought of Richard in an impressive office lined with oak, seated behind a massive desk with lackeys bowing themselves in and out, but she'd never got round to thinking of what his home was like, the house he would inherit when his father died. But now, when she looked at the long facade of gray stone pierced with mullioned windows and fronted by a great carved door, she understood perfectly well that the Bowdens were from a class several echelons above her own modest one. Lady Althea was right. She should have listened to her.

She even understood why Richard had worried about his brother's associating with an entertainer. How extremely inadequate a wife she would have made even for Sean, the younger brother. The pair of stone lions couchant, roughly life-size, that guarded the outer staircase were the final straw. They looked positively *regal*.

"Don't be frightened by the cats," he said jokingly when he saw where she was looking. "Sean and I used to ride them when we were kids."

"What a large house," she said in a very small voice. She was unhappy to have to enter it, even as a guest.

He looked down at her, concerned. "We actually live in very little of it. The state rooms are virtually unused," he told her quickly. "My own apartment in London is not so grand as this. It has only a dozen rooms."

She knew this was meant to indicate their modesty, but to her, a city apartment of a dozen rooms was nearly as far-fetched as this. He took her elbow and went up the stairs. A butler was at the door.

"I can open a door, Jenkins," he said curtly. Jenkins looked offended or perhaps surprised. She thought Richard was nervous, too, to have spoken so sharply to a servant for doing his duty.

She peered timidly at a vast expanse of marble hallway, done in black and white like a giant chess board. The walls were hung in Chinese paper. There was some intricate carving in panels, and a horse-shoe staircase with a chandelier *pendant* from the ceiling. Portraits of ancestors glowered from gilt frames on both walls of the stairway. She barely had time to notice them, for Richard hustled her immediately into a drawing room. It was not the larger, statelier one to the left that they entered, but a smaller room, almost cozy, off the right of the hall. The warm gold tones of walls and upholstered settees removed that historical chill that pervaded the other parts of the house.

There was no one in the room. "Where's Lady Bowden, Jenkins?" he asked the butler.

"Your mother is in the solarium, Mr. Bowden," Jenkins solemnly replied.

"Will you tell her our guest is here, please."

Jenkins nodded his head half an inch and left. "Sit down; let's have a drink," Richard said in a falsely hearty, ill at ease way, rubbing his hands. "Sherry, wine . . . ?"

"Sherry is fine, thank you," she said, looking through the window at a rose garden in profuse bloom. "Who is the gardener in the family?" she asked.

"Those have been there since the days of Queen Anne, with a few recent additions by our gardener. That is, the fellow who tends our grounds," he added, in the tones of a confession.

"What—is she here already?" a woman's voice was heard to say from beyond the door. The voice was high-pitched, not querulous but nervous, like Richard's. "Go to the kitchen, Jenkins. See if dinner is ready. No, he wants us to have a drink first. Oh, never mind."

Richard cast a stricken glance at Laura, then moved quickly into the hallway to invite his mother into the yellow salon. She was a surprisingly small woman to have produced two such tall sons. Small and yet stately. A spritely gray head sat proudly on her well-formed shoulders. She had the body of an athlete, close-knit and vigorous. She wore jodhpurs and a hacking jacket. Riding boots were on her feet. This unusual sight made Laura wonder whether the woman was indeed Richard's mother or some chance visitor. She bore little resemblance to the *grande dame* Laura had envisioned.

"Miss Talmadge, you must forgive the looks of me. I was at the stable and couldn't get away. That cribber of your brother's has positively *eaten* his loosebox away, Dick. I'm sorry I'm late, but I had to give Duke a good scolding."

"Duke is a mare, Laura, in case you think my mother has run mad and taken to scolding a peer of the realm. And this, of course, is my mother."

"How do you do," Laura said. When no one made any reply, she began rattling on to fill the void. "Should the horse's name not be Duchess? You *did* say mare, didn't you?"

"So I did, but mother always thought the horse looked like the Duke of Braemar and called her Duke. It's a family secret, however. Braemar might not be flattered at his namesake."

It was hardly likely Laura would tell a secret. "Mum's the word," she assured them, bewildered.

"Do you ride, my dear?" was Lady Bowden's next statement.

"Not since I was a child. I used to have a pony and cart."

"But that is not riding, my dear. It is *driving*," the lady told her bluntly.

"Richard tells me we have something in common. You are interested in the organ, I think?" Laura asked tentatively.

"Organ? What organ?" the lady asked, frowning at her son.

"The organ we are donating to the church," he said.

"It is the first *I* have heard of it. I thought the organ was for Miss Talmadge."

"Oh, no! He bought it *from* me," Laura told her.

"Really? How very odd. But why did you sell it? Dick says you play the organ."

"Let's have that glass of sherry," Richard suggested in an imperative voice.

"I always have Scotch before dinner. Have for thirty years. You are acting very oddly today, Dick. I want my Scotch. I shall have it in my room while I change."

"I'll tell Jenkins to get it," Richard said, and fled the room, hot on his mother's heels.

There was a muted colloquy behind the door, with whispered, berating phrases from the son and what sounded like a distracted apology from the mother. When he returned, he suggested a tour of the rose garden till dinner was ready. "That is, unless you would prefer to drink your sherry. . . ." he said when she looked in confusion towards the sherry tray.

"Whatever you like," she said.

"By all means, let us go into the garden," he decided, and bolted for the door.

When his mother came downstairs again, she was wearing a dark street-length dress, and a long strand of pearls. She looked questioningly to her son, as though seeking his approval. He nodded in satisfaction, and they all went to the table.

It was a large table, with only the three of them

seated at one end. An expanse of white linen stretched beyond, long enough to hold another dozen settings without crowding. It was a fairly simple meal, but served on Wedgwood porcelain with sterling silver worn smooth by many years of use. Three crystal goblets were at each place.

"Take these away," Richard said curtly to the servant, then countermanded his own order. "Leave us one each," he said irritably.

"We're having lamb. I hope you like lamb, Miss Talmadge," Lady Bowden said, again with a glance for approval at her son.

"Yes, I like it very much."

"Oh, good. And asparagus. My asparagus has done well this year. In the conservatory, I mean."

"Are you interested in gardening?" Laura asked, feeling uncomfortable in this unsettling atmosphere.

"Not at all. I am interested in horses—breeding, training, and riding them. You don't ride, you say?"

"No, I don't."

"Pity."

A silence fell and stretched ominously as courses were served.

When it was finally broken, all three opened their mouths at once. It was the eldest who took precedence. "Dickie has got a horse entered at Ascot this year," she said.

"How nice. Do you think he'll win?" Laura asked.

"*He?* My dear, only *fillies* run at Ascot," Lady Bowden told her with a little laugh. "*She* will win, certainly."

"Laura is hardly likely to know that. She has told you *twice* she is not interested in horses," Richard said stiffly.

It was a perfectly wretched meal for Laura. Every

attempt at communication between herself and Lady
Bowden was doomed to flounder. They hadn't a
single interest in common. The older lady inquired
whether Laura knew a few families from her old
neighborhood, but Laura could claim no familiarity
with any of the lords named.

As soon as possible, she thanked the hostess for
her hospitality and asked timidly of Richard when he
planned to return to London.

"Immediately!" he answered with great enthusi-
asm.

They spoke little on the way home. What few
remarks they exchanged were mainly compliments
from Laura on Hazelhurst and random questions
about the organ from Richard. She had never felt so
remote from him.

"You're quiet this evening," he said, hoping to
draw her out.

"I was just thinking."

"Sad thoughts, to judge by your expression. Was it
that bad?" he asked ruefully.

"Oh, no! Hazelhurst is beautiful. It must be
wonderful to . . . to fit in. You know what I mean.
So much elegance."

"Fitting in is really a question of people, not
things, and you can hardly call mother elegant."

"It's pretty obvious I didn't fit in with her either,"
she said, trying to disguise her profound regret. She
had hardly dared hope that Richard had bought the
organ in an effort to renew their relationship but
now, she realized that he'd taken her home to his
mother to determine how she would adjust to his
life. He had been that serious about her, had
actually considered marrying her, but this day had
surely shown him it would never work.

She had felt like a fish out of water at his house—
and that was even with his going out of his way to
smooth her path, limiting the size and grandeur of
the party, and coaching his mother. Among his
family, his father and aunts and uncles, it would be
much worse. Her mind couldn't conceive of all those
lords and ladies his mother mentioned so casually.
She would just have to forget him, she decided, and
gave a deep sigh.

"You fit in just fine with me, Laura," he said,
lifting his eyes from the road to take a short look at
her.

What did that mean? That they could go on seeing
each other in a casual way—be friends? She'd rather
not see him at all.

He left her at her door, thanking her for her
trouble, and said he hoped they would meet again
soon.

She shook her head. "Let's just leave it at this. I'm
glad we're friends again."

"We were never *friends,* Laura," he said with an
enigmatic smile and was gone.

Upon entering her own flat, she was struck by how
very shabby it must have appeared to a man who
called Hazelhurst home. But to her it was familiar
and comfortable, if not grand. She put on a record in
an effort to distract her thoughts. It wasn't likely to
do so when she rifled through her stacks to find a
rendition of "La Vie en Rose." She leaned back with
her eyes closed and relived the stormy course of their
affair from its inception to its sorrowful conclusion.
No, they had never been friends, but they had been
very passionate enemies. A tear scalded her eye,
oozing slowly down her cheek as she sat regretting
what might have been.

Chapter Ten

On Monday evening he phoned her at her flat. Her first thought was that there was some trouble with the new organ.

"No, the organ is fine. It's the organist who is at fault. Our minister is enchanted with it. He wants to put on a small concert for the parishioners on Sunday to show it off. Mr. Everett, of course, will not be in command of the instrument by that time. I was wondering if *you* might be cajoled into doing it for us. I don't want to burden you with a great deal of preparation, but if you would play some of the traditional hymns you play at St. Peter's, we would be very appreciative."

A mixture of emotions warred within her. There was, of course, some disappointment that the call was purely business. She was also reluctant to return to the precincts of his ancestral home. It might be possible too that he had in mind another of those appalling meals at Hazelhurst with his mother. She did feel a desire to play the organ, so beautiful and new, and she seldom had the opportunity to play a *real* organ nowadays. Silence grew while she considered these things.

"Are you busy on Sunday?" he asked.

"No. That is, you know I play at St. Peter's in the morning, but I could probably get down to your church by the afternoon. What time is the concert?"

"For whenever you can come. Evening, if necessary. Naturally I would drive you down and home again. Your brother Francis and his wife might be interested in coming along."

"I'm sure they would."

"Will you come then? It's presumptuous of me to ask it, but I don't know anyone else who could show the gift off for us."

Both his tone and statements were lacking in any personal significance. It was a job, or rather a charitable donation of an afternoon. It would be too mean to refuse. The Bowdens had donated an organ that cost several thousand pounds. The least she could do was to play a short concert for them.

"Yes, I'll do it. Let's set the time now. Your minister will want to put an ad in the paper or put up some notices, I imagine. I'll be playing to an empty church if he doesn't."

"How about three o'clock?" he suggested.

"That's fine."

"I'll call for you and your family a couple of hours earlier. There will be a small reception afterward, some light refreshment."

"It sounds lovely. See you next Sunday."

"We could get together before that, if you want to

discuss the program. I'm not trying to tell you what to play, but . . ."

"If you have any suggestions, by all means tell me now. I'll go over to St. Peter's to practice one day this week. I'd planned to play the hymns I usually play there, with maybe something from Bach or Haydn thrown in to show off the organ—something classical but not strictly speaking sacred organ music."

"You'll know better than I what to play. It's very kind of you to oblige me *again*."

"Oh, well, a minister's sister you know, I can hardly refuse such a request."

"You've found out my trick," he said, and laughed.

After this one hopeful statement, he soon rang off, and she sat looking at the phone. She thought it must have cost Richard something in pride to ask her this favor. During the week she made out her program and went once to play it through at St. Peter's. Francis and Mavis agreed to attend the concert. It was decided they would go to Laura's flat after lunch on Sunday to make it easier for Bowden to pick them up.

"What are you wearing?" Mavis asked Laura.

"Something modest, since it's a church function."

She chose the white street-length dress worn for her own graduation earlier that season. It was white organza with a three-quarter sleeve, a fitted waist, and full skirt. The neck was high. She wore her mother's gold locket with it. At the last minute she decided to wear a hat, a wide-brimmed leghorn bought on impulse and seldom worn.

"Doesn't she look nice, Francis? So old-fashioned and sweet," Mavis praised.

Richard came to the door of the flat. They were all ready and waiting, so that he was not even asked to sit down. He wore a light suit and did not look either old-fashioned or sweet—or even like a man on his way to church. He looked the fashionable business-man he was.

Laura didn't see how the conversation during the trip could be anything but strained with such an ill-matched group. She didn't take much part in it herself. It was mainly the men who spoke, and the women who listened, but it wasn't as awkward as Laura had feared. They discussed church attendance, the diminishing congregation, and the reasons for it. Francis had an opportunity to air his views on how the church should take a more active part in community life, and in this manner attract the interest of the youth, so important for the continuation of the church in the future.

Richard agreed with some of his views, but not automatically. He thought form and ritual were important too. "I believe impressive church cere-monies should be done up in a memorable style. Christenings, marriages, deaths—they only happen to each of us once, and if they are to have signifi-cance, they ought to be carried out with all the pomp and circumstance that can be arranged. I know when *I* marry, I want a large church wedding, my bride in a white gown, *Lohengrin*—the works."

"You must have Laura play for it," Francis said jokingly.

Richard glanced at her only briefly, but there was a curious light in his eyes. "I hope she'll be there," he said enigmatically.

Laura went up to the choir loft as soon as they arrived, to arrange her music. Richard introduced

Francis and Mavis to the pastor and gave them a tour
of the church. Glancing over the railing, Laura saw
Lady Bowden being shown up the aisle. Sean was
with her. Later Richard joined them. He ushered
Mavis and Francis into his family's pew before
entering. It was as incongruous a group as she had
ever seen sitting together in one place.

But she had little time to ponder it. She had to get
her concert prepared and make sure that everything
was in proper order. The pastor gave a short introduction, publicly thanked the Bowdens for their gift,
and her for having come down from London to play
for them. He mentioned that she was a graduate of
the Academy, and "active in the musical life of
London." She trusted he was unaware of her
activities at the Chez Nous.

She played without nervousness once she got
started, the notes swelling to fill the church. It was
pure pleasure to have this wonderful instrument
beneath her fingers, responding to her touch, her
command. It was always marvelous to her how
simple vibrations of the air could so enthrall her and
the audience too. They sat, silently appreciative.
The hour sped away like minutes. As the last chord
diminished and vanished, the minister stepped to the
center of the church to say there would be a small
reception at Hazelhurst.

All the peace of the afternoon was shattered.
Richard hadn't said Hazelhurst was to be the scene
of the reception. She thought it would occur here in
the church hall. She went down the staircase, wishing it were possible for her and Francis and Mavis to
return immediately to London, but of course the
host of the reception could hardly take them away
before his party was over. She realized Richard had

gone to considerable pains to make the trip smooth and pleasant. The car he was driving that day, for instance, was not his regular car. He had hired or borrowed a sedan for the occasion.

Richard was waiting for her below and took her to be presented to various groups of friends and to receive their compliments on her performance. Throughout this interval he kept his hand on her elbow in a proprietary way. Sean came to say hello and told her he enjoyed the music but preferred the tunes she played at the club in London.

"The woman they got to replace you isn't nearly so good. I took Sun Lee around to the place last week. Sun Lee is a friend of mine. She's a very talented actress."

"Richard mentioned her, I believe. A Eurasian girl, isn't she?"

"Yes, extremely talented, or will be, when I finish teaching her English. She doesn't have a speaking part in her present film."

"You'd better go home and see that everything is ready for the reception," Richard told him.

Before many minutes had passed, they were all speeding down the highway to Hazelhurst. "We are lucky the weather held up. Mother is having the do outside," Richard mentioned.

"A garden party! How lovely!" Mavis exclaimed. "We should have one at our church, Francis."

"That is women's work, my dear. *You* arrange it, if you wish."

"I see you have a male chauvinist in the family," Richard said quietly to Laura.

A tent had been set up in the park at Hazelhurst. Throngs of sedately outfitted men and women walked to and fro, chatting. Lady Bowden advanced to Richard's group as soon as she spotted them.

"My dear Miss Talmadge, how beautifully you played. There were tears in my eyes, and I *never* cry. You must be proud of her," she added, turning to take Francis's hand.

"You've met Laura's brother and his wife," Richard said with a slight but noticeable emphasis on Laura's name.

"You will want to chat with Reverend Willis, our pastor," Lady Bowden said, searching the throng for him. "He's bound to be here somewhere. Meanwhile, I want you to meet my cousins."

Several cousins, friends, and neighbors were met that afternoon. It was obvious at a glance they were from the same level of society as Richard. Their clothing, their manners, even their accents showed it, but with Richard's hand on her elbow, drawing her forth to talk about her music, Laura found it possible to talk to them. They were not really toplofty at all, once you got past the initial introduction. The gentlemen in particular seemed very eager for her acquaintance. An inordinate number of them were suddenly interested in organ music, and knew a dozen spots in London they were eager to take her to, to indulge their mutual hobby.

"Why don't I just jot down your phone number, and I'll give you a call?" suggested a Mr. Exeter.

"Laura is in the phone book," Richard said quickly, and piloted her in another direction.

"I'm not in the book!" she reminded him.

"I know it. You wouldn't want that rackety fellow bothering you. A deadly bore."

"Exeter is charming, Dick!" his mother pointed out.

The other subject of conversation was horses. Lady Bowden's friends actually did call her Tally-ho. A dozen times the name rang out, causing people to look around in confusion. Later Richard left Laura with his mother and went to speak to other guests.

"What a splendid afternoon wasted, what, Tally-ho?" one red-faced man complained. "We don't get many days so fine as this. How soon will this do be over? We might get in a gallop yet, before the sun sets."

"I fully intend to, but first there is one more thing I must do. I promised Dick. Laura, my dear," she ran on, turning to her, "you must come up and meet Richard's father. He's bedridden, you know, or he would be here to meet you himself. He's very eager for your acquaintance."

Her being gracious to one who had done the family a small service wasn't unusual. However, asking her upstairs to meet Sir Greville went beyond graciousness. She had to wonder why this was being done.

Lady Bowden chatted on while they went in through the French doors of a library and up to the master bedroom. "You must have thought me a perfect ninny on Friday when you were here. Richard made me so nervous with all his orders. I'm not usually the distracted female who greeted you on that occasion, Laura. It's only that in general Richard doesn't care *how* I act, and when he told me exactly what to serve and what to wear and even what to *say*—well, naturally I could not remember *everything*. I don't think I made a *complete botch* of it, however, do you?"

"Not at all," Laura said.

"He called me long distance—that rattled me. It

was my forgetting that he was buying the organ that angered him, I suspect. I would have remembered it if that cribber of Sean's hadn't acted up that day. Ah, here we are."

"Is that you, Tally-ho? Come in to see me," a man's voice called.

"We're coming. We're coming!" she called, hastening forward to push Laura into the room before her.

She took little notice of the paneled room, noticing only that it was large and well-windowed. The form in the bed drew her attention. He was an old man. Sir Greville must have married late or begun his family late at least. He was in his mid- or late seventies. His hair was white, his skin not much darker, but a pair of mischievous brown eyes lent him a lively air.

"Greville, you wanted to meet Richard's friend," Lady Bowden said. "Laura Talmadge. She plays the organ."

"Very well, too, so Dick tells me," the man said, reaching out his hand to shake hers. "You're prettier than your picture," he added, regarding her closely. "Of course it was only a picture of a picture," telling her obliquely that what he referred to was the tabloid version of the fracas at the club.

Lady Bowden cleared her throat. "Dick said not to mention that, my dear," she reprimanded gently.

"There's no point keeping secrets in your own family. We all know he made a flaming jackass of himself. I am happy to see the gel is worth it. You are very pretty, my dear. You'll do. You'll do."

"We'd better leave now," Lady Bowden said to Laura. "My husband is under doctor's orders not to get excited. A pretty blonde always excites him more than is good for him. Be a good boy now, Greville, and go to sleep," she ordered, and drew Laura out of the room. She stopped and heaved a weary sigh.

"Now what else was I supposed to do? Oh, yes, take you back to the library," she said, ticking off her duties on her fingers. "I'm sure we shall be great friends," she said as they descended. "Pity you don't ride, but then Dick hardly bothers with it nowadays."

"I shouldn't think he would have much time," Laura said.

"Dear me, no, he hasn't time for anything. I am surprise he ever found time to ask. . . . Well, well, here he is. Speak of the devil. I've done just as you said, Dick. Your papa likes Laura very much. May I go now? Orwell and I plan to sneak off for a ride before the sun sets."

"That might be a good idea, Mama," Richard said with a repressive frown at his chattering mother.

"Tally-ho!" she chirped, and darted out the door. Richard took Laura's hand and walked into the library. The garden party wasn't visible from this area. They looked out at terraced gardens with granite statuary guarding the corners.

"Why did you want me to meet your father?" she asked.

"He wanted to meet *you*. He particularly asked to."

"I can't imagine why," she said, feeling shy.

"Can't you?" he asked softly, taking her other hand in his and looking down at her. "He has enough curiosity to want to meet the woman he hears his son speak of so often, I expect. Naturally he was upset by the stories he read in the tabloids. I assured him you weren't a barroom blonde at all, but

I wanted him to see you for himself. Not that his disapproval would have deterred me from . . . that is . . ."

She remained unhelpfully silent. "You know what I am trying to say," he continued. "You have every reason to despise me. I wouldn't blame you if you did. I misread your character, and I do truthfully think you've misread mine. I don't usually go around insulting women or jumping to vile conclusions and abusing them. I'm afraid plain old green-eyed jealousy was the culprit. I wanted so much for you to be . . . as you are. I couldn't believe fate had really answered my wishes. You were too good to be true. And the circumstances under which we met were questionable, to say the least."

"Let's blame it on Sean." Laura tried to interject a lighter note through the tears that were clogging her throat. "He didn't want me to be a plain girl. He wanted a glamorous . . ."

"He wanted a barroom blonde and convinced himself and me he had found one. If only *I* had been the one to discover you at the club first, this whole imbroglio might have been avoided. But it's over now. Sean tells me he thinks you would make a charming sister-in-law. What do you say?"

"I don't think it would work, Richard," she said, her voice catching when she saw his expression. "We're miles apart—your way of life is so different from mine."

"We *can*, Laura," he insisted. "This doesn't mean anything to me," he said, flinging an arm wildly about the room. "It's not *my* chosen way of life. I happened to have been born into it. It seems hard that I'm to be penalized for something I had no choice in."

"It won't be much of a penalty. You'll soon forget," she assured him, clamping her lips shut to still their trembling.

"I have no intention of forgetting you and couldn't if I tried. Don't you think I *tried?*" he asked, his voice tense. "Even when I thought you were a gold-digging hussy, I wanted you. I won't let you go now that I know what you're really like. By God, if we have to live in your walk-up with the good-time girls, I'll marry you. Don't use this house as an excuse."

"It's not a *house!* That's the whole problem. It's a castle, and I really don't think I can handle it."

"You won't be alone, darling. I'll be with you. Is it your visits to Hazelhurst that put you off? They were designed to do just the opposite."

"Not just that. Lady Althea was right. You need a wife who was born to all this." She looked around at the room and the garden beyond. "The court functions, lady-in-waiting, protocol. I couldn't do it."

"Lady Althea?" he asked, startled. "When did you see her?"

"She paid me a visit to tell me what a poor wife I would make for you. If you didn't put her up to it, I believe your parents did."

"Never. She doesn't get on with my mother at all, though she *did* take it upon herself to come trotting to Hazelhurst with that scandal sheet I had hoped to keep from them. Althea is living in the past. . . . What did she say, exactly?"

"That we wouldn't suit. The papers described her as a good friend of yours. Isn't she?"

"An acquaintance only. We were out a few times. I wanted a woman on my arm when I went back to the Chez Nous, and asked her. I thought you were less likely to have me tossed out if I was accompanied by such a classy lady," he grinned down at her. "Well, to be truthful, maybe I hoped jealousy worked two ways. I guess I said too much to her, let it out of the bag I was smitten. With *you*, I mean."

When Laura still looked doubtful he added, "You know that the housekeeper manages the house, darling. You can just sit and play the organ all day long, if you like. It was bought with you in mind. In fact it was just an excuse to let me go and see you again."

"It was an expensive way to say hello!"

"The church needed a new organ."

"Peters tells me you are very interested in organs and organists."

"No, only in one—you," he said, his dark eyes caressing her. "When I couldn't find you at the club, I began attending Sunday services at your church. I didn't see much of you, only on the way out. The best view is from the east aisle. I used to look up to see the stained glass lighting your profile when you played the last hymn. Many a Sunday I lingered there, pretending I had dropped a hymnal, so I could watch you. When you cut me dead at the club, and when you never acknowledged my apology, I had to invent some new strategy. Has it worked?" he asked bluntly, with a glance half-hopeful, half-fearful, and all eager worry.

"I better say yes, before you buy me the Albert Hall," she answered, her voice unsteady. The image before her became blurry, but she realized it was from tears of joy, easily blinked away. The image fell into sharper focus—Richard, his eyes glowing with love. How often she had imagined this magical moment when all their difficulties were swept away. She shuddered to think how close she had come to losing him. He folded her in his arms, safe and warm and loved.

"I was a heartbeat away from telling you all this the day I bought the organ, but I wanted to make my next offer here, at Hazelhurst," he said, his lips close to her ear.

"Hoping to discourage me?" she teased.

"No, letting you know what you were in for. I didn't want any more surprises. This time, we'll do it right. It has to last till death do us part."

"Are you *sure,* Richard?"

"I've never been so sure of anything in my life. The last weeks haven't been worth living without you. I was going slowly insane without even a decent *look* at you. I need more than a look," he added, lowering his lips to hers.

They met in a gentle touch that was exquisitely tender and exhilarating. Her mind reeled to consider how her life would change, but with Richard beside her, she would cope. It was better to take on too much than too little, and without him, there was nothing.

IT'S YOUR OWN SPECIAL TIME

*Contemporary romances for today's women.
Each month, six very special love stories will be yours
from SILHOUETTE. Look for them wherever books are sold
or order now from the coupon below.*

$1.50 each

☐ 5 Goforth	☐ 28 Hampson	☐ 54 Beckman	☐ 83 Halston
☐ 6 Stanford	☐ 29 Wildman	☐ 55 LaDame	☐ 84 Vitek
☐ 7 Lewis	☐ 30 Dixon	☐ 56 Trent	☐ 85 John
☐ 8 Beckman	☐ 32 Michaels	☐ 57 John	☐ 86 Adams
☐ 9 Wilson	☐ 33 Vitek	☐ 58 Stanford	☐ 87 Michaels
☐ 10 Caine	☐ 34 John	☐ 59 Vernon	☐ 88 Stanford
☐ 11 Vernon	☐ 35 Stanford	☐ 60 Hill	☐ 89 James
☐ 17 John	☐ 38 Browning	☐ 61 Michaels	☐ 90 Major
☐ 19 Thornton	☐ 39 Sinclair	☐ 62 Halston	☐ 92 McKay
☐ 20 Fulford	☐ 46 Stanford	☐ 63 Brent	☐ 93 Browning
☐ 22 Stephens	☐ 47 Vitek	☐ 71 Ripy	☐ 94 Hampson
☐ 23 Edwards	☐ 48 Wildman	☐ 73 Browning	☐ 95 Wisdom
☐ 24 Healy	☐ 49 Wisdom	☐ 76 Hardy	☐ 96 Beckman
☐ 25 Stanford	☐ 50 Scott	☐ 78 Oliver	☐ 97 Clay
☐ 26 Hastings	☐ 52 Hampson	☐ 81 Roberts	☐ 98 St. George
☐ 27 Hampson	☐ 53 Browning	☐ 82 Dailey	☐ 99 Camp

$1.75 each

☐ 100 Stanford	☐ 114 Michaels	☐ 128 Hampson	☐ 143 Roberts
☐ 101 Hardy	☐ 115 John	☐ 129 Converse	☐ 144 Goforth
☐ 102 Hastings	☐ 116 Lindley	☐ 130 Hardy	☐ 145 Hope
☐ 103 Cork	☐ 117 Scott	☐ 131 Stanford	☐ 146 Michaels
☐ 104 Vitek	☐ 118 Dailey	☐ 132 Wisdom	☐ 147 Hampson
☐ 105 Eden	☐ 119 Hampson	☐ 133 Rowe	☐ 148 Cork
☐ 106 Dailey	☐ 120 Carroll	☐ 134 Charles	☐ 149 Saunders
☐ 107 Bright	☐ 121 Langan	☐ 135 Logan	☐ 150 Major
☐ 108 Hampson	☐ 122 Scofield	☐ 136 Hampson	☐ 151 Hampson
☐ 109 Vernon	☐ 123 Sinclair	☐ 137 Hunter	☐ 152 Halston
☐ 110 Trent	☐ 124 Beckman	☐ 138 Wilson	☐ 153 Dailey
☐ 111 South	☐ 125 Bright	☐ 139 Vitek	☐ 154 Beckman
☐ 112 Stanford	☐ 126 St. George	☐ 140 Erskine	☐ 155 Hampson
☐ 113 Browning	☐ 127 Roberts	☐ 142 Browning	☐ 156 Sawyer